The
ARABIAN
NIGHTS

The
ARABIAN
NIGHTS

With an Introduction by ORTON LOWE

ILLUSTRATED

Color Illustrations by Donald E. Cooke

HOLT, RINEHART AND WINSTON

NEW YORK

Made especially for
J. G. FERGUSON PUBLISHING COMPANY

Made in the United States of America
L. C. Card #61–8855

Introduction

TALES from a wonderful realm of enchantment, a realm of Oriental magic wherein almost anything is likely to happen are included in this edition of THE ARABIAN NIGHTS. The first thing you know you suddenly see magic ships, or valleys of diamonds, or palaces rise out of the desert, or princes change into beasts. The fine part of it all is that you can go on to another story just as good as the previous one. Of course if you want to read every one of the tales from this realm of enchantment you will need to read a huge book once known as *Tales of a Thousand Nights and One Night* but now generally called *Arabian Nights' Entertainments*. This is a fascinating collection of tales, as those selected for this volume will lead you to expect.

"This Book of Rocs,
Sandalwood, ivory, turbans, ambergris,
Cream tarts and lettered apes and calenders,
And ghouls and genies"———
is a book I liked when I was a country schoolboy in Pennsylvania. And I like it now as well as I did once upon a time. Some day I want to go back to the spot in the valley of Jacobs Creek in Westmoreland County where I first chanced to read these wonderful tales of a thousand nights and one night.

There I expect to grow young again, for I know where Aladdin's lamp is hidden, and I shall be able to go to my castles in Spain whenever I like. I know just where the enchanted horse of ebony and ivory is stabled, and then I can ride over and back across the ocean at will and never once fall into the water, for I remember exactly on which shoulder of the horse is the very screw to prevent this. Again, I recall where the Roc's nest is, and if I want a more modern way to go to the lands beyond the sea than by that of magic lamp or enchanted horse, I shall strap myself to one of the bird's toes with a cord made from my turban and I'll be flown across as any birdman would.

An English poet who wrote the lines I have quoted speaks of

the *Arabian Nights'. Entertainments* as the "gallantest and best
in all the full-shelved libraries of Romance—The sole unparalleled
Arabian Nights!" The great Scottish story-writer, Robert Louis
Stevenson, always thought of THE ARABIAN NIGHTS as the best
of any storybook.

"One night," he says, "I brought back with me the Arabian
Entertainments in the fat old double-columned volume. I was
just well into the story of the Hunchback, I remember, when my
clergyman-grandfather (a man we counted pretty stiff) came in
behind me. I grew blind with terror. But instead of ordering
the book away, he said he envied me. Ah, well he might!"

You will sometime read the story of Marjorie Fleming, a little
Scottish girl who was a great friend of Sir Walter Scott and
who was a great reader for her age. She wrote letters about what
she read and what she thought. In one of her letters she tells of
rooming with her sister and of being perfectly willing to lie at the
foot of the bed so she could be "continually at work reading the
Arabian Nights." Enough words have been used to tell how a
person will read with eagerness these wonderful Eastern stories,
so let us see how they came about and how they were brought
from Arabia to old and young readers in Europe.

The people of Arabia were learned and cultured long before
the people of Europe were and long before America was discovered.
They lived amid desert surroundings and desert climate—sunny
days, palm trees, bazaars, perfumeries. They did not hurry.
They took plenty of time to bargain whenever they traded.
Above all they told stories after the tents had been pitched for
the night. In the telling of those stories they applied figurative
language and verses of poetry to everyday topics or to topics
dealing with other lands and other people. As a result of this
manner of life the Arabs built up the wonderful stories that
make the folklore of their people.

A story is told of how the *Tales of a Thousand Nights and
One Night* came to be: Once there was a king named Shahrizar
who liked to have one of his wives tell him a tale after the day's
work was done. It was the custom of the King, when the story-
teller had finished with the tale, to cut off her head. One evening
a very beautiful wife named Shahrazad started to tell a tale that

did not end but managed to stop just at a very interesting point. The King was so curious to find out what happened next that he agreed to let Shahrazad live another day. At the conclusion of the story-telling on the second day the tale had not yet ended. King Shahrizar was more curious than ever to know what happened next. So the telling went on night after night until the story ran on for a thousand nights and one night. The King thought such a good story-teller as Shahrazad ought to live, so she came off with her life. The tales that she spun so skilfully were carried to Western countries by French and English travelers.

A Frenchman named Antoine Galland put the *Tales of a Thousand Nights and One Night* into the French language over two hundred years ago. At that time he was living in Constantinople. On his return to Paris the translation was published, and the stories became so popular that Galland was himself sought out and besieged to tell the tales to eager listeners. Young men of the streets used to gather outside the window of his study and beg of him to give "just one more of the wonderful stories."

Of the English travelers who turned the tales into English the most noted have been Richard Burton, Edward William Lane, and Jonathan Scott, all of whom had learned them in Arabia. Through these translations the great wealth of the *Arabian Nights' Entertainments* has come to the people of Europe and on to the people of the United States.

These tales are enjoyed as much today as they have ever been. This edition of two dozen choice tales is made especially for boys and girls in order that they may not miss wholly the pleasure of "the sole, unparalleled Arabian Nights."

—ORTON LOWE

Contents

List of Illustrations

The Story of
Ali Baba and
the Forty Thieves

IN an old town of Persia there lived two brothers named Cassim and Ali Baba.

Cassim married a wife who owned a fine shop and some land, and he became one of the richest men in the whole town.

Ali Baba married a wife who was as poor as himself, and lived in a very humble house. He earned his living by cutting wood in the forest and carrying it about the town on three donkeys to sell.

One day Ali Baba went to the forest, and had nearly finished cutting as much wood as his donkeys could carry, when he saw a thick cloud of dust rising high in the air. It seemed to be coming toward him. He looked at it attentively and distinguished a great company of men on horseback, riding rapidly into the woods.

Fearing that they might be robbers, he left his donkeys and quickly climbed up into a large tree with thick leafy branches. Here he could see everything that passed without being seen.

The robbers rode up to this very tree, and there dismounted. Ali Baba counted forty of them. Each horseman took the bridle off his horse and tied it to a tree. Then they took their traveling bags, which were so heavy that Ali Baba thought they must be filled with gold and silver.

The captain of the thieves, with a bag on his shoulder, came close to a rock at the roots of the tree in which Ali Baba had hidden himself. Then he called out, "Open, Sesame!" Instantly a door in the rock opened, and the captain and all his men quickly passed in. Then the door closed again. They stayed there for a long time. Meanwhile, Ali Baba was compelled to wait in the tree, as he was afraid some of them might see him if he left his hiding place.

At length the door opened, and the forty thieves came out. The captain stood at the door until all his men had passed out. Then Ali Baba heard him say, "Shut, Sesame!" Each man then bridled his horse and rode away.

Ali Baba did not come down from the tree at once because he thought the robbers might have forgotten something, and come back. He watched them as long as he could, and did not leave the tree for a long time after he had lost sight of them. Then, remembering the words the captain had used to open and shut the door, he made his way to it and called out, "Open, Sesame!" Instantly the door flew wide open!

Ali Baba expected to find only a dark cave, and he was much astonished at seeing a fine large room, dug out of the rock, and higher than a man could reach. It received its light from a hole in the top of the rock. In it were all sorts of rare fruits, bales of rich merchandise, silks and velvets, and great heaps of money, both silver and gold, some loose and some in large leather bags. The sight of all these things almost took Ali Baba's breath away.

But it did not take him long to decide what he should do. He went boldly into the cave. As soon as he was there the door shut, but he knew the secret by which to open it, and this gave him no fear. Leaving the silver, he turned to the gold, which was in the bags. When he had gathered enough to load his three donkeys, he brought them to the rock, loaded them, and covered the sacks of gold with wood so that no one would suspect anything. Before he left, he said, "Shut, Sesame!" and the door closed.

Ali Baba took the road to the town and, when he reached home, drove his donkeys into the yard and shut the gate with great care. Then he threw off the wood, carried the gold into the house, and piled it up before his wife, who was sitting upon the couch.

When he told the whole story of the cave and the forty thieves, his wife rejoiced with him and began to count the money, piece by piece. "What are you doing?" said Ali Baba. "You do not know what you are undertaking. You never could count all of it. I will dig a pit to bury it in. It is not safe to leave it here."

"You are right, husband," she replied, "but we should know about how much there is. I will go and borrow a small corn measure and, while you are digging the pit, I will find how much there is."

Away she ran to the home of her brother-in-law, Cassim, who lived but a short distance away. Cassim was not at home, so she begged his wife to lend her a measure for a few minutes. "I will with pleasure," said Cassim's wife.

She went to find a measure, but knowing how poor Ali Baba was, she was curious to know what kind of grain his wife wanted to measure. So she put some tallow under the measure where she was sure it would not be seen.

The wife of Ali Baba returned home and, placing the measure on the heap of gold, filled it over and over again until she had measured the whole of it. By this time Ali Baba had dug the pit for the gold, and while he was burying it, his wife went back with the measure to her sister-in-law, not noticing that a piece of gold had stuck to the bottom of it.

As soon as the measure had been returned, Cassim's wife looked at the bottom, and was astonished to see a piece of gold sticking to it. "What!" she said, "Ali Baba measures his gold! Where did he get so much?"

When her husband came home, she said, "Cassim, you think you are rich, but Ali Baba must have far more wealth than you. He does not count his gold as you do. He measures it." Then she showed him the piece of money she had found sticking to the bottom of the measure.

Far from feeling glad at the good fortune of his brother, Cassim grew so jealous of Ali Baba that he passed almost the whole night without closing his eyes. Next morning before sunrise he went to see his brother. "Ali Baba," said he, "you pretend to be a poor beggar, and yet you measure your money in a corn measure." Then Cassim showed him the piece of gold his

He had forgotten the secret words.

wife had given him, and added, "How many pieces have you like this one that my wife found sticking to the bottom of the measure yesterday?"

From this speech Ali Baba knew that Cassim and his wife must suspect what had happened. So, without showing the least sign of surprise, he told Cassim by what chance he had found the den of thieves. He also told him where it was and offered to share the treasure with him.

"I certainly expect this," replied Cassim in a haughty tone, "otherwise I will go and inform the police of it."

Ali Baba even told him the words he must say to open and close the door of the cave. Cassim made no further inquiries of Ali Baba. However, he determined to seize the whole treasure, and set off next morning before break of day with ten mules carrying large hampers which he intended to fill. He took the road that Ali Baba had pointed out, and soon found the rock and the tree.

When he cried, "Open, Sesame!" the door opened. He entered, and it closed again. The greedy Cassim spent half the day in feasting his eyes on the sight of so much gold, but he remembered that he had come to take away as much as his ten mules could carry. Therefore, he filled his sacks and, coming to the door, he found that he had forgotten the secret words, and instead of saying, "Open, Sesame," he said "Open, Barley." But the door, instead of flying open, remained closed. He named various other kinds of grain, but he could not think of the right one, and the door did not move.

Cassim was not prepared for this. He threw down the bags he had loaded himself with, and walked distractedly up and down the cave.

The thieves returned to their cave a little before noon; and when they were within a short distance of it and saw the mules with the hampers standing about the rock, they were much surprised. They drove away the ten mules, which fled into the forest. Then the captain and his men dismounted and went toward the door, with their sabers in their hands. The captain said, "Open, Sesame!" and the door opened.

From the inside of the cave, Cassim heard the horses trampling on the ground and did not doubt that the thieves had come, and that his death was near. Resolving to make an effort to escape, he placed himself near the door, ready to run out as soon as it should open. The words, "Open, Sesame," were scarcely pronounced before it opened, and he rushed out with such violence that he threw the captain to the ground. However, he could not escape the other thieves, who slew him with their sabers.

On entering the cave the thieves found the sacks that Cassim had left near the door, but they could not imagine how he had been able to get in.

He was struck with horror.

They decided to divide the body of Cassim
into four parts, and place them in the cave to
frighten away anyone else who might have the
boldness to break in. Then, leaving it well
secured, they mounted their horses and rode
away.

In the meantime, the wife of Cassim was in
the greatest uneasiness. When night came, and
her husband did not return, she went in the
utmost alarm to Ali Baba, and said, "Brother,
I believe that Cassim has gone to the forest.
He has not come back, and I fear some accident
may have befallen him."

Ali Baba did not wait to be urged to go and
seek for Cassim. He immediately set out with
his three donkeys, and went to the forest. As
he drew near the rock he was astonished to see
that blood had been shed near the cave. When
he reached the door, he said, "Open, Sesame!"
and it opened. He was struck with horror to find
the quartered body of his brother near the
entrance. He decided to carry it home, so wrap-
ping it up, he placed it on one of his donkeys
and covered it with sticks to conceal it. He
quickly loaded the other two donkeys with sacks
of gold, putting wood over them as before.
Then he commanded the door to close.

After waiting in the forest until nightfall,
he took the road to the city and returned without
being seen. When he reached home, he left the
two donkeys that were laden with gold for his
wife to unload. Then, having told her what had
happened to Cassim, he led the other donkey to
his sister-in-law.

Ali Baba knocked at the door, which was
opened by Morgiana, who was a clever female
slave. When he had entered the court, he took
from the back of the donkey the wood and the
body. "Morgiana," he said, "I have to ask you
to keep a deep secret! Here is the body of your
master. We must bury him as if he had died a

natural death. Now, let me speak to your mistress."

Morgiana went to call her mistress, and Ali Baba told her all that had happened. "Sister," added he, "here is a sad affliction for you, but we must contrive to bury my brother as if he had died a natural death. Then we shall be glad to offer you a shelter under our own roof."

The widow of Cassim decided that she could not do better than consent. She therefore dried her tears and thanked Ali Baba for his kindness.

Ali Baba and Morgiana went to a druggist and asked for a particular kind of medicine to be used in dangerous illness. The druggist gave her the medicine and asked who was ill in her master's family. "Ah!" exclaimed she with a deep sigh, "it is my worthy master, Cassim himself. He can neither speak nor eat!"

Meanwhile, as Ali Baba and his wife were seen in the course of the day going backwards and forwards to the house of Cassim, no one was surprised on hearing in the evening the piercing cries of his widow and Morgiana, announce his death.

At a very early hour the next morning, Morgiana betook herself to the stall of a cobbler named Mustapha. Coming up to him, she wished him a good day and put a piece of gold into his hand, saying: "Baba Mustapha, you must take your sewing tackle and come with me. But you must let me put a bandage over your eyes when we come to a certain street."

At these words Baba Mustapha began to shake his head. "No," said he, "you want me to do something wrong."

But, putting another piece of gold into his hand, Morgiana said, "I want you to do nothing wrong. Only come with me, and fear nothing."

Baba Mustapha then followed Morgiana. When they reached the street she had mentioned, she bound a handkerchief over his eyes and led him to Cassim's house. She did not remove the bandage until he was in the chamber where the body lay. Then she said, "Baba Mustapha, I have brought you here, that you might sew these pieces together. Lose no time, and when you have finished, I will give you another piece of gold."

When Baba Mustapha had finished his work, Morgiana blindfolded his eyes again before he left the chamber, and having given him a third piece of money, she led him to the place where she had first put on the handkerchief. Then she left him to return to his house. And so the body of Cassim was prepared for burial, which took place the same day.

"No," said he, "you want me to do something wrong."

Ali Baba and Morgiana followed the body to the grave, but his widow remained at home to lament and weep with her neighbors, according to the usual custom. At the time of the burial, all her women friends came to her house and, joining their cries to hers, filled the air with sounds of woe. Thus the manner of Cassim's death was so well hidden that no one in the city had any suspicion of it.

When the forty thieves came back to their cave, they found the body of Cassim was gone, and with it much of their treasure. "We have been discovered," said the captain, "and we shall lose our lives if we are not very careful. All that we can now tell is that the man whom we killed in the cave knew the secret of opening the door. But he was not the only one. Another must have found it out, too. Having slain one, we must not let the other escape. One of you must go to the city, without arms and in the dress of a traveler, and try to discover the name and the residence of the man we killed."

The thief who agreed to carry out this plan disguised himself so that no one could tell who he was. Then he set out at night, and entered the city just as day was dawning. When he entered the square, only one shop was open. and that was the shop of Baba Mustapha, the cobbler.

Baba Mustapha was seated on his stool, with his awl in his hand, ready to begin his work. The thief went up to him and wished him good morning. "My good man," said he, "you rise early to your work. You must find it hard to see clearly at this early hour."

"Whoever you are," replied Baba Mustapha, "you do not know much of me. Old as I am, I have good eyes; and so you would have said if you had known that not long ago I sewed up a

"Come, here is another piece of gold."

dead body in a place where there was no more
light than we have now."

The thief felt great satisfaction at having
so soon found a man to give him the very news
he wanted. "A body?" said he, with attempted
surprise. "Why sew up a dead body?"

"Oh!" replied Baba Mustapha, "I know; you
want me to tell you all about it, but you shall
not know another word."

Thereupon the thief drew out a piece of gold
and, putting it into Baba Mustapha's hand, said,
"I have no desire to know any secret. The only

thing I ask of you is to come with me and show me the house where you sewed up the dead body."

"I cannot," replied Baba Mustapha, "and I will tell you why. They took me to a certain street, there blindfolded my eyes, and then led me to the house. When I had finished, I was led back the same way."

"But," said the thief, "you must remember the way you went after your eyes were covered. Come with me. I will put a bandage over your eyes, and we will walk together along the same streets and follow the same turnings. Come, here is another piece of gold."

The two pieces of gold tempted the cobbler. "I cannot say," said he, "that I exactly remember the way they took me, but, since you insist, I will do my best!"

So Baba Mustapha got up to go with him, and, without shutting up his shop, he led the thief to the spot where Morgiana had put the bandage over his eyes. Here the thief, who had a handkerchief ready, tied it over the cobbler's eyes, and walked by his side, partly leading him and partly being led by him, till he stopped.

The cobbler was exactly in front of the house which formerly belonged to Cassim, and where Ali Baba now lived. Before he took the

The thief quickly made a mark on the door.

bandage from his eyes, the thief quickly made
a mark on the door with some chalk he had for
the purpose. When he had taken it off, he asked
him if he knew to whom the house belonged.
Baba Mustapha replied that he did not live in
that part of the town, and could not tell him.
As the thief found he could learn nothing more
from Baba Mustapha, he thanked him for the

trouble he had taken, and left him to return to
his shop, while he himself took the road to the
forest.

Soon after this, Morgiana had occasion to
go into the street and saw the mark which the
thief had made on the door of Ali Baba's house.
"What can this mark mean?" thought she.
"Has anyone a spite against my master, or has
it been done only for fun? In any case, it will
be well to guard against the worst that may
happen."

Several of the doors, both above and below
her master's, were alike, so she took some chalk
and marked them in the same manner. Then
she went in without saying anything of what
she had done either to her master or mistress.

The thief in the meantime arrived at the
forest, and told the success of his journey.
They all listened to him with great delight, and
the captain, after praising him, said, "Comrades, we have no time to lose. Let us arm ourselves and depart. We will enter the city separately and meet in the great square before we
go to find the house with the chalk mark."

Thus the thieves went to the city in parties
of two or three without causing any suspicion.
The thief who had been there in the morning
then led the captain to the street in which he

had marked the house of Ali Baba. When they reached the first house that had been marked by Morgiana, he pointed it out, saying that was the one. But as they continued walking on, the captain saw that the next door was marked in the same manner. At this the thief was quite confused, and knew not what to say. And they found four or five other doors with the same mark.

The captain, in great anger, returned to the square, and told the first of his men he met to tell the rest that they had lost their labor, and that nothing remained but to return to the forest.

When they had reached the forest, the captain declared that the mistaken thief deserved death, and his head was at once cut off by his companions.

Next day another thief went to the city, found the cobbler, who led him to Ali Baba's house, and marked the door with red. A short time afterwards, Morgiana went out and, seeing the red mark, did not fail to make a similar red mark on all the neighboring doors.

The thief, when he returned to the forest, boasted of his success, and the captain and the rest repaired to the city with as much care as before. The captain and his guide then went

to the street where Ali Baba resided, but the
same thing occurred as before.

Thus they were obliged to return again to
the forest, where the second thief had his head
cut off.

The next day the captain himself went to
the city and, with the help of Baba Mustapha,
found the house of Ali Baba. But he did not
waste any time in making marks on it. He examined it well, and walked up and down before
the house until it was impressed upon his mind.

Thereupon he returned to the forest. He
told the thieves he had made sure of the house
and had made a plan that they must help him
to carry out.

First he sent them into the neighboring
towns and villages to buy nineteen mules and
thirty-eight large leather jars for carrying oil.
One of the jars must be full of oil, and all the
others empty.

In two or three days the thieves returned,
and the captain made an armed man enter each
jar and then close the lid. Thus they appeared
full of oil. And he also rubbed the oil on the
outside of the jars.

The mules were soon loaded with the thirty-
eight jars, and then the captain led the way to
the city. He arrived there about an hour after

He was much astonished at seeing a fine large room

The captain himself went to the city.

sunset, and went straight to the house of Ali Baba. He found Ali Baba at the door, enjoying the cool evening air. He stopped his mules. "Sir," said he, "I have brought this oil from a great distance to sell tomorrow in the market. I do not know where to go to pass the night. If it will not cause you too much trouble, do me the favor to take me under your roof."

Although Ali Baba had seen the man who now spoke to him in the forest, and had heard his voice, yet he had no idea that this was the captain of the forty thieves disguised as an oil merchant. "You are welcome," said he, and immediately made room for him and his mules. Then Ali Baba called a slave and ordered him

to put the mules in the stable and to give them
some hay and corn. He also took the trouble
of going into the kitchen to ask Morgiana to
get supper for his guest and to prepare his room.

When Ali Baba went into the kitchen to
speak to Morgiana, the captain of the thieves
went into the court as if he were going to the
stable to look after his mules.

Having told Morgiana to look to his guest,
and to see that he wanted nothing, Ali Baba
added, "Tomorrow before daybreak I shall go
to the bath. Take care that my bathing linen
is ready, and have some good broth for me when
I return." After giving these orders he went
to bed.

In the meantime, the captain of the thieves
went to give his people orders. Beginning with
the first jar and going to the whole number, he
said, "When I shall throw some pebbles from my
chamber, do not fail to rip open the jar from
top to bottom with your knife."

Having done this, he returned to the house,
ate his supper, and was shown to his chamber.
To avoid any suspicion, he put out the light and
lay down in his clothes, ready to rise as soon as
he had taken his first sleep.

Morgiana did not forget Ali Baba's orders.
She prepared his linen for the bath and gave it

to a slave who was not yet gone to bed. Then she put the pot on the fire to make the broth, but while she was skimming it, the lamp went out. There was no more oil in the house and she had no candles. At last she went to take some oil out of one of the jars in the court.

As she drew near to the first jar, the thief who was concealed within, said in a low voice, "Is it time?"

Although he spoke softly, Morgiana heard him. Any other slave except her would have made a great uproar at finding a man in the jar instead of some oil. But Morgiana imitated the voice of the captain and answered, "Not yet." She approached the next jar, and the same question was asked. She went on to them all in turn, making the same answer to the same question, until she came to the last, which was full of oil.

By this means, Morgiana discovered that her master, who supposed he was giving a night's lodging to an oil merchant, had given shelter to thirty-eight robbers. She quickly filled her oil-can from the last jar and returned to the kitchen. After putting some oil in her lamp and lighting it, she took a large kettle and went again into the court to fill it with oil from the jar. This done, she brought it back again, put it over the fire, and made a great blaze under

She poured boiling oil into each jar.

it with some wood. As soon as the oil boiled, she took the kettle and poured into each jar, from the first to the last, enough boiling oil to stifle and destroy the robbers.

This being done without any noise, she returned to the kitchen and shut the door. Then she blew out the light and remained silent at the kitchen window to see what would happen.

Before she had waited a quarter of an hour, the captain of the robbers awoke. He got up, opened the window and looked out. All was dark and silent. He gave the signal by throwing the pebbles, many of which fell on the jars with a rattling sound. He listened, but heard nothing. He became uneasy at the delay, and threw some more pebbles down. They all struck the jars, yet nothing moved, and he was at a loss to account for it. He went down into the court in great alarm and with as little noise as possible. He went up to the first jar, and was just going to ask if the robber in it were asleep, when he smelled burning oil. He went to the next jar, and to the others in turn, and discovered that all his men were dead. Terrified at this, he jumped over the garden gate and made his escape.

When Morgiana saw that all was still and that the captain of the thieves did not return, she was overjoyed at the success of her plan. Then she returned satisfied to her room and was soon fast asleep.

Ali Baba went to the bath before daybreak followed by his slave. He was totally unaware of the events which had taken place in his house during his sleep. When he returned from the bath, he was surprised to see the jars of oil still standing in the court. He asked Morgiana why the oil merchant had not gone to the market.

"My good master," said Morgiana, "may God preserve you and all your family. You will soon know the reason if you will take the trouble to come with me."

Ali Baba followed Morgiana, and when she had shut the door, she took him to the first jar and bade him look in and see if it contained oil. He did as she desired and, seeing a man in the jar, he hastily drew back and uttered a cry of surprise.

"Do not be afraid," said she, "the man you see there will not do you any harm. He has attempted it, but he will never hurt you or any one else."

"Morgiana!" exclaimed Ali Baba, "what does all this mean?"

"I will explain," replied Morgiana, "but be careful not to arouse the curiosity of your

She took him to the first jar and bade him look in.

neighbors. It is very important that you should keep the matter secret. Now come and look in all the other jars."

Ali Baba examined all the rest of the jars until he came to the last, which contained the oil, and he noticed that its oil was nearly all gone. At last he said, "And what is become of the merchant?"

"The merchant," replied Morgiana, "is no more a merchant than I am." Then she described the marks made upon the door and the way in which she had copied them. "You see," said she, "that a plot has been made by the thieves of the forest. There are not more than three of them left, but you will do well to be on your guard against them, so long as even one remains."

Ali Baba was full of gratitude and replied, "I will reward you as you deserve before I die. I owe my life to you. From this moment I give you your liberty and will soon do still more for you."

Meanwhile the captain of the forty thieves had returned to the forest, full of rage and determined to revenge himself on Ali Baba.

Next morning he awoke at an early hour, put on a merchant's dress, and returned to the city. He took a shop and brought some wares to sell in it. This shop was exactly opposite that which had belonged to Cassim, and was now occupied by the son of Ali Baba.

The captain of the thieves soon made friends with the son of Ali Baba who was young and good-natured. He often invited the young man to sup with him and gave him many rich gifts. When Ali Baba heard of it, he decided to make some return for this kindness of the merchant. He little thought that the pretended merchant was really the captain of the thieves. So one day he asked the merchant to do him the honor of supping and spending the evening at his house.

"Sir," replied he, "I am grateful for your kindness; but I must beg you to excuse me. I never eat of any dish that has salt in it, so I could not eat at your table."

"If this is your only reason," replied Ali Baba, "it need not prevent you from coming to supper with me. The bread which is eaten in my house does not contain any salt; and I promise you there shall be none in the meat which is served to you."

So Ali Baba went into the kitchen, and asked Morgiana not to put any salt into the meat she was going to serve for supper. Morgiana could not help being annoyed at this and asked, "Who is this man who cannot eat salt? Your supper will be good for nothing without it."

"Do not be angry," replied Ali Baba. "He is a good man. Do what I wish."

Morgiana obeyed, but she felt some curiosity to see this man who did not eat salt. On looking at the pretended merchant, she instantly knew him to be the captain of the robbers in spite of his disguise. She saw that he had a dagger hidden under his dress.

"I am no longer surprised," said she to herself, "that this villain will not eat salt with my master*. He is his greatest enemy, and means to kill him, but I will prevent it!"

When supper was ended, the captain of the forty thieves thought that the time had come for revenging himself on Ali Baba. But Morgiana did not allow him time to carry out his wicked plans. Dressed as a dancer, she wore a girdle round her waist, to which was fastened a dagger. Her face was hidden by a very handsome mask. When she had thus disguised herself, she made a courtesy, and performed several dances. At length she drew out the dagger and plunged it into the heart of the robber.

Ali Baba and his son were terrified at this. "Wretch!" exclaimed Ali Baba, "what have you done? You have ruined me and my family forever."

"What I have done," replied Morgiana, "is not for your ruin but for your safety." Then, opening the robber's robe, she showed Ali Baba the dagger which was concealed under it. "Look carefully," said she, "and you will recognize the pretended oil merchant and the captain of the forty thieves! Do you now see why he refused to eat salt with you?"

Ali Baba now saw that he owed Morgiana for thus saving his life a second time. He cried

---

* In Oriental countries, eating salt together is a pledge of friendship.

out, "Morgiana, some time ago I gave you your liberty and at the same time promised to do more for you at some future time. That time has now arrived, and I present you to my son as his wife and welcome you as a daughter."

A few days after this, Ali Baba's son and Morgiana were married. After the marriage, Ali Baba decided to again visit the cave of the forty thieves. On reaching it, he dismounted and went up to the door, and repeated the words, "Open, Sesame." At once the door opened, and he entered the cave. He found that no one had been in it from the time that the pretended merchant had opened his shop in the city. He therefore knew that the whole band of thieves had been killed, and that he was the only person who knew the secret of the cave.

From that time, Ali Baba and his son, whom he took to the cave and taught the secret, enjoyed its riches and lived in great happiness and comfort to the ends of their lives.

The Story of Sindbad the Sailor

I N the reign of the Caliph Haroun al-Raschid there dwelt in Bagdad a poor porter named Hindbad, who often had to carry heavy burdens which he could scarcely support. One very hot day he was laboring along a strange street and, overcome by fatigue, he sat down near a great house to rest. The porter complimented himself upon his good fortune in finding such a pleasant place, for while he sat, there reached his ears sweet sounds of music and his senses were also soothed by sweet smells. Wondering who lived in so fine a house, he inquired of one of the servants.

"What!" said the man, "do you not know that Sindbad the Sailor, the famous voyager who has sailed around the world, lives here?"

He sat down near a great house to rest.

"Alas!" replied Hindbad, "what a difference there is between Sindbad's lot and mine! Yet what greater merit does he possess that he should prosper and I starve?"

Now Sindbad happened to overhear this remark; and, anxious to see a man who expressed such strange views, he sent for Hindbad. Accordingly Hindbad was led into the great hall, where there was a sumptuous repast spread and a goodly company assembled. The poor porter felt very uncomfortable until Sindbad bade him draw near and, seating him at his right hand, gave him food and drink, serving him himself.

When the repast was over, Sindbad asked him why he complained of his condition. "My lord," replied Hindbad, "I confess that my fatigue put me out of humor and occasioned me to utter some indiscreet words, which I beg you to pardon."

"Do not think I am so unjust," resumed Sindbad, "as to resent such a complaint. But that you may know that my wealth has not been gained without labor, I recite the history of my travels for your benefit. I think that, when you have heard it, you will acknowledge how wonderful have been my adventures." Sindbad then related the story of his first voyage as follows:

THE FIRST VOYAGE

When still a very young man I inherited a large fortune from my father and at once set about amusing myself. I lived luxuriously and soon found that money was decreasing, while nothing was added to replace the expenditure. Quickly seeing the folly of my ways, I invested the remainder of my fortune with some mer-

chants of Bussorah and joined them in their
voyage, which was toward the Indies by way of
the Persian Gulf.

In our voyage we touched at several islands
where we sold or exchanged our goods. One
day, whilst under sail, we were becalmed near a
small island but little elevated above the level of
the water and resembling a green meadow. The
captain ordered his sails to be furled and permitted such persons as were so inclined to land.
Of this number I was one.

But while we were enjoying ourselves in eating and drinking and recovering ourselves from
the fatigue of the sea, the island on a sudden
trembled and shook us terribly.

The trembling of the island was perceived on
board the ship, and we were called upon to re-
embark speedily or we should all be lost. What
we took for an island proved to be the back of
a sea monster. The nimblest got into the sloop,
others betook themselves to swimming, but for
myself I was still upon the back of the creature
when he dived into the sea. I had time only to
catch hold of a piece of wood that we had
brought out of the ship to make a fire. Meanwhile, the captain, having received those on
board who were in the sloop and taken up some
of those that swam, resolved to improve the

favorable gale that had just risen. Hoisting his
sails he pursued his voyage, so that it was impossible for me to recover the ship.

Thus was I exposed to the mercy of the
waves. I struggled for my life all the rest of
the day and the following night. By this time
I found my strength gone and despaired of saving my life, when, happily, a wave threw me
against an island. I struggled up the steep
bank by aid of some roots and lay down upon
the ground half dead, until the sun appeared.
Then, though I was very feeble both from hard
labor and want of food, I crept along to find
some herbs fit to eat. I had the good luck not
only to procure some but likewise to discover a
spring of excellent water which contributed
much to recover me.

As I advanced farther into the island, I was
not a little surprised and startled to hear a voice
and see a man who asked me who I was. I related to him my adventure. Taking me by the
hand, he led me into a cave where there were
several other people, no less amazed to see me
than I was to see them.

I partook of some provisions which they
offered me. I then asked them what they did in
such a desert place, to which they answered that
they were grooms belonging to the Maharajah,

I struggled up the steep bank.

sovereign of the island, and that they were about
to lead the king's horses back to the palace.
They added that they were to return home on
the morrow, and, had I been one day later, I must
have perished, because the inhabited part of the
island was at a great distance and it would have

been impossible for me to have got thither without a guide.

When the grooms set out, I accompanied them and was duly presented to the Maharajah, who was much interested in my adventure and bade me stay with him as long as I desired.

Being a merchant, I met with men of my own profession. I particularly inquired for those who were strangers, that perchance I might hear news from Bagdad, or find an opportunity to return, for the Maharajah's capital is situated on the seacoast and has a fine harbor where ships arrive daily from the different quarters of the world. I frequented also the society of the learned Indians and took delight in hearing them converse; but withal, I took care to make my court regularly to the Maharajah, and conversed with the governors and petty kings, his tributaries, that were about him. They put a thousand questions respecting my country; and I, being willing to inform myself as to their laws and customs, asked them concerning everything which I thought worth knowing.

One day as I was at the port, the ship in which I had set sail arrived, and the crew began to unload the goods. I saw my own bales with my name upon them. Going up to the captain

I took care to make my court regularly to the Maharajah.

I said, "I am that Sindbad whom you thought to be dead, and those bales are mine."

When the captain heard me speak thus, "Heavens!" he exclaimed, "whom can we trust in these times? There is no faith left

among men. I saw Sindbad perish with my own
eyes, as did also the passengers on board, and
yet you tell me you are that Sindbad. What
impudence is this? To look on you, one would
take you to be a man of honesty, and yet you
tell a horrible falsehood in order to possess yourself of what does not belong to you."

"Nevertheless, I am Sindbad the Sailor," I
insisted. "You must believe me. I speak nothing but the truth."

I spoke earnestly and brought to his remem-
brance a number of things that had happened
on our voyage with the merchants of Bussorah.

After much discussion, the captain was convinced of the truth of my words and, having
seen me identified by members of the crew, he
handed me over my goods, congratulating me
upon my escape.

I took out what was most valuable in my
bales and presented them to the Maharajah,
who, knowing my misfortune, asked me how I
came by such rarities. I acquainted him with
the circumstance of their recovery. He was
pleased at my good luck, accepted my present,
and in return gave me one much more considerable. Upon this, I took leave of him and went
aboard the same ship, after I had exchanged my
goods for the commodities of that country. We

passed by several islands, and at last arrived at
Bussorah, whence I came to this city with goods
which I sold for one hundred thousand sequins.

Sindbad stopped here and ordered the musi-
cians to proceed with their concert, which the
story had interrupted. The company continued
enjoying themselves till the evening, and it was
time to retire. Then Sindbad sent for a purse
of one hundred sequins and, giving it to the
porter, said, "Take this, Hindbad, return to your
home, and come back tomorrow to hear more of
my adventures."

The porter went away, astonished at the
honor done and the present made him. Arrayed
in his best apparel, he returned to Sindbad's
house next day and was welcomed heartily.
When all the guests had arrived, dinner was
served. After dinner Sindbad, addressing himself to the company, said: "Gentlemen, be
pleased to listen to the adventures of my second
voyage. They deserve your attention even more
than those of my first voyage."

Upon which everyone held his peace, and
Sindbad proceeded with his narrative.

The
Second Voyage of
Sindbad

I INTENDED, after my first voyage, to spend the rest of my days at Bagdad; but it was not long ere I grew weary of a quiet life, and, therefore, I set out a second time upon a voyage. We embarked on board a good ship and set sail. We traded from island to island and exchanged commodities with great profit. One day we landed at an island covered with several sorts of fruit trees, but we could see neither man nor animal. We went to take a little fresh air in the meadows, along the streams that watered them. While some diverted themselves with gathering flowers and others sought fruits, I took my wine and provisions and sat down near a stream betwixt two high trees, which formed a thick shade. I made a good meal and afterwards fell asleep. I cannot tell how long I slept, but when I awoke the ship was gone.

I regretted not being content with the produce of my first voyage, that might have sufficed me all my life. But all this was in vain. My repentance too late. Not knowing what to do, I climbed up to the top of a lofty tree, whence I looked about on all sides to see if I could discover anything that could give me hopes. When I gazed over the land I beheld something white. Coming down, I took what provisions I had left and went toward it, the distance being so great that I could not distinguish what it was.

As I approached, I thought it to be a white dome of a great height and extent. When I came up to it, I touched it and found it to be very smooth. I went around to see if it was open on any side, but saw it was not and that there was no climbing up to the top as it was so smooth. It was at least fifty paces round.

By this time the sun was about to set, and all of a sudden the sky became dark as if it had been covered with a thick cloud. I was much astonished at this sudden darkness but much more when I found it occasioned by a bird of monstrous size that came flying toward me. I remembered that I had often heard mariners speak of a miraculous bird called a roc, and conceived that the great dome which I so much admired must be its egg.

In a short time, the bird alighted and sat over the egg. As I perceived her coming, I crept close to the egg so that I had before me one of the legs of the bird, which was as big as the trunk of a tree. I tied myself strongly to it with my turban, in hopes that the roc next morning would carry me with her out of this desert island.

After having passed the night in this condition, the bird flew away as soon as it was daylight and carried me so high that I could not discern the earth. She afterwards descended with so much rapidity that I lost my senses. But when I found myself on the ground, I speedily untied the knot, and had scarcely done so, when the roc, having taken up a serpent of great length in her bill, flew away.

The spot where it left me was encompassed on all sides by mountains that seemed to reach above the clouds, and so steep that there was no possibility of getting out of the valley. This was a new perplexity. When I compared this place with the desert island from which the roc had brought me, I found that I had gained nothing by the change.

As I walked through this valley, I perceived it was strewn with diamonds, some of which

I tied myself strongly to it with my turban.

were of a surprising size. I took pleasure in looking upon them, but shortly saw at a distance some objects that greatly diminished my satisfaction and which I could not view without terror, namely, a great number of serpents so monstrous that the least of them was capable of swallowing an elephant. They retired in the daytime to their dens, where they hid themselves from the roc, their enemy, and came out only in the night.

I spent the day in walking about in the valley, resting myself at times in such places as I thought most convenient. When night came on, I went into a cave and secured the entrance, which was low and narrow, with a great stone to preserve me from the serpents, but not so far as to exclude the light. I supped on part of my provisions, but the serpents, which began hissing round me, put me into such extreme fear that, you may easily imagine, I did not sleep.

When day appeared, the serpents retired, and I came out of the cave trembling. I can justly say that I walked upon diamonds without feeling any inclination to touch them. At last I sat down and, notwithstanding my apprehensions, not having closed my eyes during the night, fell asleep, after having eaten a little more of my provisions. But I had scarcely shut my eyes when something that fell by me with a great noise awakened me. This was a large piece of raw meat. At the same time, I saw several others fall down from the rocks in different places.

I had always regarded as fabulous what I had heard sailors and others relate of the valley of diamonds and of the means employed by merchants to obtain jewels thence. Now I found that they had stated nothing but the truth, for as a fact, the merchants come to this valley when the eagles have young ones, and throw great joints of meat into the valley. The diamonds, upon whose points they fall, stick to them, and the eagles, which are stronger in this country than anywhere else, pounce with great force upon those pieces of meat and carry them to their nests on the precipices of the rocks to feed their young. The merchants at this time run to their nests, disturb and drive off the eagles by their shouts, and take away the diamonds that stick to the meat.

The happy idea struck me that here was a means of escape from my living tomb. I collected a number of the largest diamonds and put them into the leather bag in which I used to carry my provisions, and which I tied to my girdle. Then I fastened one of the joints of meat to the middle of my back by means of my turban cloth, and lay down with my face to the ground.

I had scarcely placed myself in this posture when the eagles came. Each of them seized a piece of meat, and one of the strongest having taken me up with the piece of meat to which I was fastened, carried me to his nest on the top of the mountain. The merchants began their shouting to frighten the eagles; and when they had obliged them to quit their prey, one of them came to the nest where I was. He was much alarmed when he saw me, but recovering himself, instead of inquiring how I came thither, began to quarrel with me, and asked why I stole his goods.

"You will treat me," replied I, "with more civility when you know me better. Do not be uneasy. I have diamonds enough for you and myself, more than all the other merchants together. Whatever they have they owe to chance, but I selected for myself in the bottom of the valley those which you see in this bag."

I had scarcely done speaking, when the other merchants came crowding about us, much astonished to see me; but they were much more surprised when I told them the story.

They conducted me to their encampment, and there, when I opened my bag, were surprised at the largeness of my diamonds and confessed that in all the courts which they had visited they had never seen any of such size and perfection. I prayed the merchant, who owned the nest to which I had been carried (for every merchant had his own), to take as many for his share as he pleased. He contented himself with one, and that too the least of them. I pressed him to take more. "No," said he, "I am very well satisfied with this, which is valuable enough to save me the trouble of making any more voyages and will raise as great a fortune as I desire."

I spent the night with the merchants, to whom I related my story a second time for the satisfaction of those who had not heard it. I could not moderate my joy when I found myself delivered from the danger I have mentioned. I thought myself in a dream and could scarcely believe myself out of danger. When at length I reached home, I gave large presents to the poor, and lived luxuriously upon my hard-earned wealth.

Thus Sindbad ended the account of his second voyage, and, having given Hindbad another hundred sequins, asked him to come on the next day to hear his further adventures.

The
Third Voyage of
Sindbad

I SOON resolved upon a third voyage, and once more took ship at Bussorah. After we had been at sea a few weeks, we were overtaken by a dreadful storm and were obliged to cast anchor near an island which the captain had endeavored to avoid. He assured us that it was inhabited by pygmy savages, covered with hair, who would speedily attack us in great numbers.

Soon an innumerable multitude of frightful savages, about two feet high, boarded the ship. Resistance was useless. They took down our sails, cut our cable, towed the ship to land, and made us all go on shore. We went toward the interior of the island and discovered a large building. It was a lofty palace, having a gate of ebony, which we pushed open, and soon discovered a room in which were human bones and roasting spits.

Presently there appeared a hideous black man, who was as tall as a palm tree. He had but one eye, his teeth were long and sharp, and his nails like the talons of a bird. He took me up as I would a kitten, but finding I was little better than skin and bone, put me down with contempt. The captain, being the fattest of the party, was sacrificed to his appetite. When the monster had finished his meal he stretched himself upon a great stone bench in the portico and fell asleep, snoring louder than thunder. In this manner he slept till morning. In the morning he went out. Then I said to my companions:

"Do not waste time in useless sorrow; let us hurry to look for timber to make rafts."

We found some timber on the seashore and labored hard, but having no tools, it was evening before we had finished. While we were on the point of pushing the raft off the beach, our hideous tyrant returned and drove us to his palace as if we had been a flock of sheep. We saw another of our companions sacrificed, and the giant lay down to sleep as before. Our desperate condition gave us courage. Nine of us got up very softly and held the points of the roasting spits in the fire until we made them red-hot. We then thrust them at once into the monster's eye. He uttered a frightful scream and, having tried in vain to find us, opened the ebony gate and left the palace.

We did not stay long behind him, but ran to the seashore, got our rafts ready, and waited for daylight to embark. At dawn we beheld our monstrous enemy, led by two giants of equal size, and followed by many others. We jumped upon our rafts and pushed them from the shore, the tide helping us. The giants seeing us likely to escape, tore great pieces of rock and, wading in the water up to their waists, hurled them at us with all their might. They sank every one of the rafts but that on which I was; thus all my companions, except two, were drowned. We rowed as fast as we could and got out of reach of these monsters.

We were at sea two days but at last found a pleasant island. After eating some fruit, we lay down to sleep but were soon awakened by the hissing of an enormous serpent. One of my comrades was instantly devoured by this terrific creature. I climbed up a tree as fast as I could, and reached the topmost branches. My remaining companion was following me, but the dreadful reptile entwined itself round the tree

and caught him. The serpent then went down and glided away.

I waited until late the next day before I ventured to descend. Evening again approached, and I gathered together a great quantity of small wood, brambles, and thorns. Having made them into fagots, I formed a circle round the tree, and fastened the uppermost to the branches of the tree. I then climbed up to the highest branches. At night the serpent came again. He could not reach the tree and, after crawling vainly round and round my little fortification until daylight, he went away.

The next day I spied a ship in full sail a long way off. With the linen of my turban I made a signal, which was perceived. I was taken on board the ship and there told the strange story of my adventures. The captain was very kind to me. He said that he had some bales of goods which had belonged to a merchant who had unintentionally left him some time ago on an uninhabited island. As this man was undoubtedly dead, he intended to sell the goods for the benefit of his relatives, and I should have the profit of selling them. I now recollected this was the captain with whom I sailed on my second voyage. I soon convinced him that I was really Sindbad, whom he sup-

The giants seeing us likely to escape, tore great pieces of rock—and hurled them at us with all their might.

With the linen of my turban I made a signal.

posed to have been lost. He was delighted at
the discovery and eagerly acknowledged that
the property was mine. I continued my voyage,

sold my goods to great advantage, and returned to Bagdad.

Having thus finished the account of his third voyage, Sindbad sent Hindbad on his way, after he had given him another hundred sequins and invited him to dinner the next day to hear the continuation of his adventures.

The
Fourth Voyage of
Sindbad

The
Fourth Voyage of
Sindbad

MY desire of seeing foreign countries rendered my pleasures at home unsatisfactory. I therefore arranged my affairs, commenced a voyage to Persia, and having bought a large stock of goods loaded a ship and again embarked. The ship struck upon a rock, and the cargo was lost. A few others and myself were borne by the current to an island on which we were surrounded by black savages and carried to their huts. The savages offered us herbs which my companions eagerly took, for they were hungry. Grief would not allow me to eat, and presently I saw that the herbs had made my comrades senseless. Rice, mixed with oil of coconuts, was then offered to us, which my companions ate greedily and grew fat. My unhappy friends were then devoured, one after

Surrounded by black savages and carried to their huts.

another, having become appetizing to the canni-
bals. But I languished so much that they did
not think me fit to eat.

They left me to the care of an old man from
whom I managed to escape. He called to me as
loud as he could to return, but I redoubled my
speed and, taking care to go a contrary way
from that which the savages had taken, I never
stopped till night.

I redoubled my speed.

At the end of seven days, on the seashore I
found a number of white persons gathering
pepper. They asked me in Arabic who I was
and whence I came, and I gave them an account
of the shipwreck and of my escape. They treated
me kindly and presented me to their king, who
treated me with great liberality.

During my stay with them, I observed that
when the king and his nobles went hunting,
they rode their horses without bridle or saddle.
With the assistance of some workmen, I made
a bridle and saddle and, having put them upon
one of the king's horses, presented the animal
thus equipped to his majesty. He was so delighted that he instantly mounted and rode
about the grounds almost the whole day. All
the ministers of state and the nobility induced
me to make saddles and bridles for them, for
which they made me magnificent presents.

The king at last requested that I would
marry and become one of his nation. From a
variety of circumstances I could not reiuse, and
he therefore gave me one of the ladies of his
Court, who was young, rich, beautiful, and vir-
tuous. We lived in the greatest harmony in a
palace belonging to my wife.

I had made a good friend of a very worthy
man who lived in this place. Hearing one day

They rode their horses without bridle or saddle.

that his wife had just died, I went to condole
with him on this unexpected calamity. We were
alone together, and he appeared to be in the
deepest grief. After I had talked with him some
time on the uselessness of so much sorrow, he
told me that it was an established law that the
living husband should be buried with the de-
ceased wife, and that within an hour he must
submit. I shuddered at the dreadful custom.

In a short time the woman was attired in
her most costly dress and jewels, and placed in
an open coffin. The procession then began, the
husband following the corpse. They ascended
to the top of an exceedingly high mountain, and
a great stone was removed, which covered the
mouth of a deep pit. The corpse was let down,
and the husband, having taken leave of his
friends, was put into another open coffin, with
a pot of water and seven small loaves, and he
was let down. The stone was replaced and they
all returned.

The horror of this was still fresh upon my
mind, when my wife fell sick and died. The
king and the whole Court, out of respect to me,
instantly prepared to assist at a similar cere-
mony with me. I restrained the feeling of despair until we arrived at the top of the mountain, when I fell at the feet of the king and
begged him to spare my life. All I said was
ineffectual, and after my wife was let down, I
also was put into the deep pit, everyone being
totally indifferent to my cries and lamentations.

I lived some days on the bread and water
which had been put into my coffin, but this supply was at length exhausted. I then wandered
to a remote part of this frightful cave and lay
down to prepare for death. I was thus wishing

only for a speedy termination of my misery, when I heard something walking and panting.

I started up, upon which the thing panted still more, and then ran away. I pursued it, and sometimes it seemed to stop, but on my approach continued to go on before me. I pursued it until at last I saw a glimmering light like a star. This redoubled my eagerness, until at last I discovered a hole large enough to allow my escape. I crept through the aperture and found myself on the seashore. I discovered that the creature was a sea monster which had been accustomed to enter at that hole to feed upon the dead bodies.

Having eaten some shellfish, I returned to the cave, where I collected all the jewels I could find in the dark. These I carried to the seashore and tied them up very neatly into bales with the cords that let down the coffins. I laid

I pursued it.

them on the beach and waited till some ship should pass.

In two days a ship came out of the harbor and passed by that part of the coast. I made a signal, and a boat took me on board. I was obliged to say that I had been wrecked; for, had they known my real story, I should have been carried back, as the captain was a native of this country.

We touched at several islands and at the port of Kela, where I found a ship ready to sail for Bussorah. Having presented some jewels to the captain who had brought me to Kela, I sailed, and at last arrived at Bagdad.

Sindbad then presented another hundred sequins to the porter and bade him honor him with his presence again next day.

The
Fifth Voyage of
Sindbad

HAVING forgotten my former perils, I built a ship at my own expense, loaded it with a rich cargo, and, taking with me other merchants, once more set sail. We were much driven about by a storm, and at length landed upon a desert island to search for fresh water. There we found a roc's egg, equal in size to the one I had seen before.

The merchants and sailors gathered round it and, though I advised them not to meddle with it, they nevertheless made a hole in it with their hatchets and picked out the young roc, piece after piece, and roasted it.

They had scarcely finished, when two of the old birds appeared in the air. We hurried on board ship and set sail, but had not gone far before we saw the immense birds approaching.

One of them let fall an enormous fragment of stone which fell into the sea close beside the ship, but the other let fall a piece which split our ship.

I caught hold of a bit of the wreck, on which I was borne by the wind and tide to an island, the shore of which was very steep. I reached the dry land and found the most delicious fruits and excellent water, which refreshed me. Farther in the island I saw a feeble old man sitting near a rivulet. When I inquired of him how he came there, he only answered by signs for me to carry him over the rivulet, that he might eat some fruit.

I took him on my back and crossed the brook, but instead of getting down, he clasped his legs so firmly round my throat that I thought he would strangle me. I soon fainted with pain and fright. When I recovered the old fellow was still sitting on my neck. He quickly made me rise up and walk under the trees, while he gathered the fruit at his ease. This lasted a long time.

One day, while carrying him about, I picked up a large gourd called a calabash, and, having cleared out the inside, I pressed into it the juice of grapes. Having filled it, I left it for several days, and at length found that it became excellent wine. I drank of this and, for a while, forgot my sorrows so that I began to sing with cheerfulness.

The old man made me give him the calabash, and liking the flavor of the wine, he drank it off, soon became intoxicated, fell from my shoulders, and died in convulsions.

I hastened to the seaside and presently found the crew of a ship. They told me I had fallen into the hands of the Old Man of the Sea, and was the first person that had ever escaped. I sailed with them; and the captain, when we landed, took me to some persons whose employment was to gather coconuts. We all took up stones and pelted the monkeys that were at the very top of the coconut trees, and these animals in return pelted us with coconuts.

When we had obtained as many as we could carry, we returned to the town. I soon obtained a considerable sum by the coconuts I thus gathered, and at length sailed for my native land.

When he had thus finished his story Sindbad presented Hindbad with a hundred sequins, as before, and entreated him to present himself at the usual hour the next day.

The
Sixth Voyage of
Sindbad

At the expiration of another year, I prepared for a sixth voyage. This proved very long and unfortunate, for the pilot lost his course and knew not where to steer. At length he told us we must inevitably be dashed to pieces against a rock which we were fast approaching. In a few moments the vessel was a complete wreck. We saved our lives, our provisions, and our goods.

The shore on which we were cast was at the foot of a mountain which it was impossible to climb, so that I shortly beheld my companions die one after another. There was a frightful cavern in the rock, through which flowed a river. To this, in a fit of desperation, I resolved to trust myself. I went to work and made a long raft. I loaded it with bales of rich stuffs and large

66

The pilot lost his course.

pieces of rock crystal, of which the mountain was in a great measure formed. I went on board the raft, and the current carried me along in darkness many days, and at last fell asleep.

I cannot tell how long I remained insensible,
but when I revived, I was surprised to find myself in an extensive plain on the brink of a river.
My raft was tied amidst a great number of
negroes. I got up as soon as I saw them and
saluted them. They spoke to me, but I did not
understand their language. I was so transported with joy that I cried aloud in Arabic,
expressing my gratitude to God.

One of the blacks who understood Arabic,
hearing me speak thus, came toward me and
said, "Brother, pray tell us your history, for it
must be extraordinary. How did you venture
yourself upon this river and whence did you
come?"

I begged of them first to give me something
to eat and assured them I would then satisfy
their curiosity. They gave me several sorts of
food, and when I had satisfied my hunger, I related all that had befallen me, which they listened to with attentive surprise. Having
brought a horse, they conducted me to their
king that he might hear so remarkable a story.

We marched till we came to the capital of
Serendib, for it was in that island I had landed.
The blacks presented me to their king. I approached his throne and saluted him as I used
to do the kings of the Indies, that is to say, I

I went on board the raft.

prostrated myself at his feet. The prince ordered me to rise, received me with an obliging air, and made me sit down near him.

He first asked me my name, and I answered, "People call me Sindbad the Voyager, because of the many voyages I have undertaken, and I am a citizen of Bagdad."

I then narrated all my adventures without reserve and, observing that he looked on my

jewels with pleasure, and viewed the most remarkable among them one after another, I fell
prostrate at his feet and took the liberty to say
to him, "Sir, not only my person is at your
majesty's service, but the cargo of the raft, and
I would beg of you to dispose of it as your
own."

He answered me with a smile, "Sindbad, instead of taking from you, I intend to add presents worthy of your acceptance."

All the answer I returned was a prayer for
the prosperity of that nobly-minded prince and
commendations of his generosity and bounty.
He charged one of his officers to take care of
me and ordered people to serve me at his own
expense. The officer was very faithful in the
execution of his commission and caused all the
goods to be carried to the lodgings provided
for me.

The capital of Serendib stands at the end of
a fine valley in the middle of the island, encompassed by mountains the highest in the world.
They are seen three days' sail off at sea. Rubies
and minerals abound. Rare plants and trees
grow there, especially cedars and coconut.
There is also a pearl-fishery in the mouth of its
principal river, and in some of its valleys are
found diamonds.

Having spent some time in the capital and visited all the places of interest around, among which is the place where Adam dwelt after his banishment from Paradise, I prayed the king to allow me to return to my own country, and he granted me permission.

He forced a rich present upon me and, when I went to take my leave of him, he gave me one much more considerable. At the same time he charged me with a letter for the Commander of the Faithful, our sovereign, saying to me, "I pray you give this present from me and this letter to the caliph, and assure him of my friendship."

The letter from the king of Serendib was written on the skin of a certain animal of great value, because of its being so scarce, and of a yellowish color. The characters of this letter were of azure, and the contents as follows:

"The king of the Indies, before whom march one hundred elephants, who lives in a palace that shines with one hundred thousand rubies, and who has in his treasury twenty thousand crowns enriched with diamonds, to Caliph Haroun al-Raschid.

"Though the present we send you be inconsiderable, receive it, however, as a brother and

a friend, in consideration of the hearty friendship which we bear for you and of which we are
willing to give you proof. We desire the same
part in your friendship, considering that we
believe it to be our merit, being of the
same dignity with yourself. We send you
this greeting as from one brother to another.
Adieu."

The present consisted firstly of one single
ruby made into a cup, about half a foot high, an
inch thick, and filled with round pearls of half
a drachm each. Secondly, the skin of a serpent,
whose scales were as large as an ordinary piece
of gold, and had the virtue to preserve from
sickness those who lay upon it. Thirdly, fifty
thousand drachms of the best wood of aloes,
with thirty grains of camphire as big as pista-
chios. And, fourthly, a female of exceeding
beauty, whose apparel was all covered over with
jewels.

The ship set sail, and after a very successful
navigation we landed at Bussorah, and thence
I went to Bagdad, where I immediately went to
deliver the king's letter to the caliph. After I
had presented myself, the caliph listened with
attention to my description of the Indies, expressed his thanks, and generously rewarded
me.

Having spoken thus, Sindbad notified that the account of his sixth voyage was at an end and presented Hindbad with another hundred sequins, urging him to return next day to hear the history of his seventh and last voyage.

THE Caliph Haroun al-Raschid one day
sent for me and told me I must bear a
present to the king of Serendib. I ventured to
protest on account of my age, but I could not
persuade him to give up his plan.

I arrived at Serendib and prayed an audience
with the king. I was conducted to the palace
with great respect, and delivered to the monarch
the Caliph's letter and present. The present
consisted of the most ingenious and valuable
works of art, with which the king was exceedingly delighted, and he was also pleased to
acknowledge how much he esteemed my serv-
ices.

When I departed, the monarch bestowed on
me some rich gifts; but the ship had not long
been at sea, before it was attacked by pirates

who seized the vessel and carried us away as slaves. I was sold to a merchant.

When my master found that I could use the bow and arrow with skill, he took me upon an elephant, and carried me to a vast forest in the country. My master ordered me to climb a high tree and wait there until I saw a troop of elephants pass by. I was then to shoot at them, and if one of them fell, I was to go to the city and give the merchant notice. Having given me these directions and a bag of provisions, he left me.

On the morning of the second day, I saw a great number of elephants. I succeeded in shooting one of them, upon which the others went away. I returned to the city and told my master, who praised my work.

We went back to the forest and dug a hole in which the elephant was to remain until it decayed and left the teeth free. I continued this trade nearly two months and killed an elephant almost every day.

One morning all the elephants came up to the tree in which I was and trumpeted dreadfully. One of them fastened his trunk round the tree and tore it up by the roots. I fell with the tree; the animal took me up with his trunk and placed me on his back. Then, at the head of his troop, he brought me to a place where he gently laid me on the ground, and they all went away. I discovered that I was upon a large broad hill, covered all over with the bones and teeth of elephants, and was soon convinced that this was their burying place.

I reached the city once more. My master thought I was lost, for he had seen the torn tree, and found my bow and arrows. I told him what had happened and led him to the hill. We loaded the elephant on which we had come, and thus collected more teeth than a man could have obtained in his whole life. The merchant told me that not only he himself, but the whole city, was indebted to me, and that I should return to my own country with sufficient wealth to make me happy. My patron loaded a ship with ivory, and the other merchants made me valuable presents.

I reached Bussorah and landed my ivory, which I found to be more valuable than I had expected. I set out with caravans to travel overland and at last reached Bagdad, where I presented myself to the caliph and gave an account of my embassy. He was so astonished at my adventure with the elephants that he ordered the narrative of it to be written in letters of gold and to be deposited in his treasury.

... Fastened his trunk round the tree and tore it up by the roots.

He ordered the narrative to be written in letters of gold.

Sindbad here finished the relation of his seventh and last voyage and then addressing himself to Hindbad, "Well, friend," said he, "did you ever hear of any person that suffered so much as I have done, or of any mortal that has gone through so many vicissitudes? Is it not reasonable that, after all this, I should enjoy a quiet and pleasant life?"

Hindbad drew near, kissed his hand in token of his respect, and said how insignificant were his own troubles compared with those he had heard related.

Sindbad gave him another hundred sequins and told him that every day there would be a place laid for him at his table and that he could always rely upon the friendship of Sindbad the Sailor.

The Merchant
and the Genie

HERE was formerly a merchant who possessed much property in lands, goods, and money. One day, being under the necessity of going a long journey on an affair of importance, he mounted his horse. He carried with him a wallet containing biscuits and dates, because he had a great desert to pass over where he could procure no sort of provisions. He arrived without accident at the end of his journey, and having dispatched his affairs, set out on his return.

The fourth day of his journey, he was so much distressed by the heat of the sun that he turned out of the road to refresh himself under some trees where he found a fountain of clear water. Having alighted, he tied his horse to a branch and, sitting down by the fountain, took

He found a fountain of clear water.

some biscuits and dates out of his wallet. As he ate his dates, he threw the stones carelessly in different directions. When he had finished his repast, being a good Mussulman, he washed his hands, face, and feet, and said his prayers.

Before he had finished, and while he was yet on his knees, he saw a genie of monstrous bulk advancing towards him with great fury, whirling a scimitar in his hand.

The genie spoke to him in a terrible voice: "Rise, that I may kill thee with this scimitar, as thou hast killed my son"; and accompanied these words with a frightful roar.

The merchant, being as much alarmed at the hideous shape of the monster as at his threats, answered him trembling, "Alas! how could I kill your son? I never knew, never saw him."

"Did not you, when you came hither," demanded the genie, "take dates out of your wallet and, as you ate them, throw the stones about in different directions?"

"I did all that you say," answered the merchant, "I cannot deny it."

"When thou wert throwing the stones about," resumed the genie, "my son was passing by, and thou didst throw one into his eye, which killed him. Therefore I must kill thee."

"Ah! my lord! pardon me!" cried the merchant.

"No pardon," exclaimed the genie, "no mercy. Is it not just to kill him that has killed another?"

"I agree it is," replied the merchant, "but certainly I never killed your son; and if I have, it was unknown to me, and I did it innocently; I beg you therefore to pardon me and suffer me to live."

"No, no," returned the genie, persisting in his resolution; "I must kill thee, since thou hast killed my son." Then, taking the merchant by the arm, he threw him with his face on the ground, and lifted up his scimitar to cut off his head.

When the merchant saw that the genie was going to cut off his head, he cried to him, "Allow me one word, I entreat you. Have the goodness to grant me a respite of one year to bid my wife and children adieu and to divide my estate among them. I promise you that this day twelve months I will return under these trees to put myself into your hands."

"Do you take Allah to be witness to this promise?" said the genie.

"I do," answered the merchant, "and you may rely on my oath." Upon this the genie left him near the fountain and disappeared.

When the merchant, on reaching home, related what had passed between him and the genie, his wife uttered the most piteous cries, beat her breast, and tore her hair. The children, all in tears, made the house resound with their groans; and the father, not being able to resist the impulse of nature, mingled his tears with theirs.

At last the year expired, and he was obliged to depart. He put his burial clothes in his wallet. When he came to bid his wife and children adieu, their grief surpassed description. Affected beyond measure by the parting of his dear ones, the merchant journeyed to the place where he had promised to meet the genie.

Seating himself down by the fountain, he awaited the coming of the genie, with all the sorrow imaginable. While he languished under this painful expectation, an old man leading a hind appeared and drew near him. After they had saluted each other, the old man inquired of him why he was in that desert place.

The merchant related his adventures, to the old man's astonishment.

While the merchant and the old man who led the hind were talking, they saw another old man coming towards them, followed by two black dogs. When he was informed of the merchant's adventure, he declared his resolve to stay and see the issue.

In a short time they perceived a thick vapor, like a cloud of dust raised by a whirlwind, advancing towards them. When it had come up to them, it suddenly vanished, and the genie appeared. Without saluting them, he went to the merchant with a drawn scimitar, and, taking him by the arm, said, "Get thee up, that I may kill thee, as thou didst my son." The merchant and the two old men began to lament and fill the air with their cries.

When the old man who led the hind saw the genie lay hold of the merchant, and about to kill him, he threw himself at the feet of the monster, and kissing them, said to him, "Prince of genies, I most humbly request you to suspend your anger, and do me the favor to listen to the story of my life, and of the hind you see; and if you think it more wonderful and surprising than the adventure of the merchant, I hope you will pardon the unfortunate man one half of his offence."

The genie took some time to deliberate on this proposal, but answered at last, "Well, then I agree."

Whereupon the old man with the hind told his story.

The Old Man
and the Hind

THIS hind you see is my wife, whom I married when she was twelve years old. We lived together for twenty years without having any children.

My desire of having children induced me to adopt the son of a slave. My wife, being jealous, cherished a hatred for both the child and his mother, but concealed her aversion so well that I knew nothing of it till it was too late.

While I was away on a long journey, she applied herself to magic and, by her enchantments, she changed the child into a calf and the mother into a cow, and gave them both into the charge of my farmer.

On my return, I inquired for the mother and child. "The slave," said she, "is dead; and as for your adopted son, I know not what is become of him. I have not seen him these two months."

I was afflicted at the death of the slave; but as my son had only disappeared, I was in hopes he would shortly return. However, eight months passed, and I heard nothing of him. When the festival of the great Bairam* was to be celebrated, I sent to my farmer for one of the fattest cows to sacrifice. He accordingly sent me one. I bound her; but as I was going to sacrifice her, she bellowed piteously, and I could perceive tears streaming from her eyes. This seemed to me very extraordinary and, finding myself moved with compassion, I could not find it in my heart to give her a blow but ordered my farmer to get me another.

My wife, who was present, was enraged at my tenderness and resisting an order which disappointed her malice. She cried out, "What are you doing, husband? Sacrifice that cow. Your farmer has not a finer nor one fitter for the festival."

Out of deference to my wife, I ordered the farmer, less compassionate than myself, to sacrifice her. When he flayed her, he found her to be nothing except bones, though to us she seemed very fat.

---

* Or Beiram. One of the great Mohammedan festivals.

"Take her away," said I to him, "dispose of her in alms or any way you please; and if you have a very fat calf, bring it me in her stead."

He returned with a fat calf, which, as soon as it beheld me, made so great an effort to come near me, that he broke his cord, threw himself at my feet, with his head against the ground, as if he meant to excite my compassion and implore me not to be so cruel as to take his life.

I was more surprised and affected with this action than with the tears of the cow, and, addressing my wife, said: "Wife, I will not sacrifice this calf, and pray do not you oppose me."

The wicked woman had no regard to my wishes but urged me until I yielded. I tied the poor creature and, taking up the fatal knife, was going to plunge it into the calf's throat, when turning his eyes, bathed with tears, in a languishing manner towards me, he affected me so much that I had not the strength to kill him. I let the knife fall and told my wife positively that I would have another calf to sacrifice. I pacified her a little by promising that I would sacrifice him at the feast of Bairam the following year.

The next morning my farmer desired to speak with me alone. He told me that his daughter, who had some skill in magic, desired

He in an instant recovered his natural form.

to see me. When she was admitted, she informed me that while I was on my journey my wife had changed the slave into a cow and the child into a calf. She could not restore the slave, who, in the shape of a cow, had been sacrificed, but she could give me my adopted son again and would do so, if she might have him for a husband, and also punish my wife as she deserved.

When I had given my consent to these proposals, the damsel took a vessel full of water, pronounced over it words that I did not understand, and threw the water over the calf. He in an instant recovered his natural form.

"My son, my dear son," cried I, immediately embracing him with a transport of joy, "this young maid has removed the horrible charm by which you were enchanted and I doubt not but in acknowledgment you will make your deliverer your wife as I have promised." He joyfully consented.

But, before they married, she changed my wife into a hind; and this is she whom you see here.

Since that time, my son is become a widower, and gone to travel. It being now several years since I heard of him, I am come abroad to inquire after him. Not being willing to trust anybody with my wife till I should return home, I thought fit to take her everywhere with me. This is the history of myself and this hind. Is it not one of the most wonderful and surprising?

"I admit it is," said the genie, "and on that account forgive the merchant one half of his crime."

When the first old man had finished his story, the second, who led the two black dogs, addressed the genie and said: "I am going to tell you what happened to me and these two black dogs you see by me. But when I have done this, I hope you will pardon the merchant the other half of his offence."

"I will," replied the genie, "provided your story surpass that of the hind." Then the second old man began.

The Old Man
and the Two
Black Dogs

G REAT prince of genies, you must know
that we are three brothers, the two
black dogs and myself. Our father, when he
died, left each of us one thousand sequins. With
that sum, we all became merchants. My brothers resolved to travel and trade in foreign
countries.

At the end of a year, they returned in abject
poverty, having, in unfortunate enterprises, lost
all. I welcomed them home and, having pros-
pered, gave each of them a thousand sequins to
start them again as merchants. After a while
they came to me to propose that I should join
them in a trading voyage. I immediately de-
clined. But after having resisted their plead-
ings five whole years, I at length yielded.

I buried the other three thousand.

When, however, the time arrived that we were to buy the goods necessary to the undertaking, I found they had spent all and had nothing left of the thousand sequins I had given to each of them. I did not, on this account, upbraid them. On the contrary, my stock being now six thousand sequins, I gave each of them a thousand and, keeping as much for myself, I buried the other three thousand in a corner of my house.

We purchased goods and, having embarked them on board a vessel which we freighted betwixt us, we put to sea with a favorable wind. After two months' sail, we arrived happily at port where we landed and had a very good market for our goods. I, especially, sold mine so well that I gained ten to one.

When we were ready to embark on our return, I met on the seashore a lady, very handsome, but poorly clad. She walked up to me gracefully, kissed my hand, and besought me with the greatest earnestness imaginable to marry her. I made some difficulty before agreeing to this proposal; but she urged so many things to persuade me that I ought not to object to her on account of her poverty and that I should have all the reason in the world to be satisfied with her conduct, that at last I yielded. I ordered proper apparel to be made for her, and after having married her according to form, I took her on board, and we set sail. I found my wife possessed so many good qualities that my love for her every day increased.

In the meantime my two brothers, who had not managed their affairs as successfully as I had mine, envied my prosperity. They suffered their feelings to carry them so far that they conspired against my life; and one night, when my wife and I were asleep, threw us both into the sea.

I had scarcely fallen into the water when she took me up and carried me to an island. When day appeared, she said to me, "You see, husband, that by saving your life I have not rewarded you ill for your kindness to me. You must know that I am a fairy and, being upon the seashore when you were going to embark, I had a mind to try your goodness and presented myself before you in disguise. You have dealt generously by me, and I am glad of an opportunity of returning my acknowledgment. But I am incensed against your brothers, and nothing will satisfy me but their lives."

I listened to this discourse with admiration.* I thanked the fairy the best way I could for the great kindness she had done me. "But, madam," said I, "as for my brothers, I beg you to pardon them. Whatever cause of resentment they have given me, I am not cruel enough to desire their death."

I then informed her what I had done for them, but this increased her indignation. She exclaimed, "I must immediately pursue those

_____
* admiration = wonder.

ungrateful traitors and take speedy vengeance on them. I will destroy their vessel and sink them into the bottom of the sea."

"My good lady," I implored, "for the sake of Heaven forbear. Moderate your anger. Consider that they are my brothers, and that we ought to return good for evil."

I pacified her by these words; and as soon as I had concluded, she transported me in a moment from the island to the roof of my own house. I descended, opened the doors, and dug up the three thousand sequins I had formerly secreted. I went afterwards to my shop, which I also opened; and was complimented by the merchants, my neighbors, upon my return. When I went back to my house, I perceived there two black dogs which came up to me in a very submissive manner. I could not divine the meaning of this circumstance which greatly astonished me. But the fairy, who immediately appeared, said, "Husband, be not surprised to see these dogs. They are your brothers."

I was troubled at this declaration and asked her by what power they were so transformed. "I did it," said she, "and at the same time sunk their ship. You have lost the goods you had on board, but I will compensate you another way. As to your two brothers, I have condemned them to remain five years in that shape. Their per-fidiousness too well deserves such a penance." Having thus spoken and told me where I might hear of her, she disappeared.

The five years being now nearly expired, I am traveling in quest of her.

Thus ended the story of the second old man, who led the two black dogs.

There was a moment's silence. Then the old man, addressing the genie, continued:

"This is my history, O prince of genies! do you not think it very extraordinary?"

"I own it is," replied the genie, "and on that account I remit the merchant the other half of the crime which he has committed against me." With these words, the genie rose and disappeared in a cloud of smoke to the great delight of the merchant and the two old men.

The merchant failed not to make due acknowledgment to his deliverers. They rejoiced to see him out of danger and, bidding him adieu, each of them proceeded on his way. The merchant returned to his wife and children and passed the rest of his days with them in peace.

The Story of
the Fisherman

THERE was an aged fisherman who was
so poor that he could scarcely earn as
much as would maintain himself, his wife, and
three children. He went every day to fish betimes in the morning, and imposed it as a law
upon himself not to cast his nets above four
times a day. He went one morning by moonlight, and, coming to the seaside, undressed
himself. There several times did he cast his net
and have a heavy haul. Yet, to his indescribable
disappointment and despair, the first proved to
be an ass, the second a basket full of stones, and
the third a mass of mud and shells.

As day now began to appear he said his
prayers, for he was a good Mussulman, and
commended himself and his needs to his Creator.
Having done this, he cast his nets the fourth

He took a knife and opened it.

time and drew them, as formerly, with great difficulty; but, instead of fish, found nothing in them but a vessel of yellow copper, with the impression of a seal upon it.

This turn of fortune rejoiced him. "I will sell it," said he, "to the founder, and with the money buy a measure of corn."

He examined the vessel on all sides and shook it, to try if its contents made any noise, but heard nothing. This circumstance, with the impression of the seal upon the leaden cover, made him think it inclosed something precious. To try this, he took a knife and opened it. He turned the mouth downwards, but nothing came out, which surprised him extremely. He placed it before him, but while he viewed it attentively, there came out a very thick smoke which obliged him to retire two or three paces back to avoid being smothered.

The smoke ascended to the clouds and, extending itself along the sea and upon the shore, formed a great mist, which we may well imagine filled the fisherman with astonishment. When the smoke was all out of the vessel, it reunited and became a solid body, of which was formed a genie twice as high as the greatest of giants. At the sight of such a monster, the fisherman would fain have fled, but was so frightened that he could not move.

The genie regarded the fisherman with a fierce look and exclaimed in a terrible voice, "Prepare to die, for I will surely kill thee."

"Ah!" replied the fisherman, "why would you kill me? Did I not just now set you at liberty, and have you already forgotten my kindness?"

"Yes, I remember it," said the genie, "but that shall not save thy life. I have only one favor to grant thee."

"And what is that?" asked the fisherman.

"It is," answered the genie, "to give thee thy choice in what manner thou wouldst have me put thee to death."

"But wherein have I offended you?" demanded the fisherman. "Is that your reward for the service I have rendered you?"

"I cannot treat thee otherwise," said the genie, "and that thou mayest know the reason, hearken to my story.

"I am one of those rebellious spirits that opposed the will of Heaven.

"Solomon, the son of David, commanded me to acknowledge his power and to submit to his commands. I refused, and told him I would rather expose myself to his resentment than swear fealty as he required. To punish me, he shut me up in this copper vessel. That I might not break my prison, he himself stamped upon this leaden cover his seal with the great name of God engraven upon it. He then gave the vessel to a genie, with orders to throw me into the sea.

"During the first hundred years of my imprisonment, I swore that if any one should deliver me before the expiration of that period, I would make him rich. During the second, I made an oath that I would open all the treasures of the earth to any one that might set me at liberty. In the third, I promised to make my deliverer a potent monarch, to be always near him in spirit, and to grant him every day three requests of whatsoever nature they might be. At last, being angry, or rather mad, to find myself a prisoner so long, I swore that if any one should deliver me, I would kill him without mercy and grant him no other favor but to choose the manner of his death. Therefore, since thou has delivered me today, I give thee that choice."

The fisherman was extremely grieved, not so much for himself, as on account of his three children, and bewailed the misery they must be reduced to by his death. He endeavored to appease the genie and said, "Alas! be pleased to take pity on me in consideration of the service I have done you."

"I have told thee already," replied the genie, "it is for that very reason I must kill thee. Make haste and tell me how you wish to die."

Necessity is the mother of invention. The fisherman bethought himself of a stratagem. "Since I must die then," said he to the genie, "I submit to the will of Heaven; but before I choose the manner of my death, I conjure you by the great name which was engraven upon the seal of the prophet Solomon, the son of David, to answer me truly the question I am going to ask you."

The genie, finding himself obliged to a positive answer by this adjuration, trembled, and replied to the fisherman, "Ask what thou wilt, but make haste."

"I wish to know," asked the fisherman, "if you were actually in this vessel. Dare you swear it by the name of the great God?"

"Yes," replied the genie, "I do swear by that great name that I was."

"In good faith," answered the fisherman, "I cannot believe you; the vessel is not capable of holding one of your feet, and how should it be possible that your whole body could lie in it?"

"Is it possible," replied the genie, "that thou dost not believe me after the solemn oath I have taken?"

"Truly not I," said the fisherman; "nor will I believe you, unless you go into the vessel again."

Upon which the body of the genie dissolved and changed itself into smoke, extending as before upon the seashore. At last, being collected, it began to re-enter the vessel, which it continued to do till no part remained out. Immediately the fisherman took the cover of lead and speedily replaced it on the vessel.

"Genie," cried he, "now it is your turn to beg my favor. I shall throw you into the sea, whence I took you, and then I will build a house upon the shore where I will reside and give notice to all fishermen who come to throw in their nets to beware of such a wicked genie as thou art, who hast made an oath to kill him that shalt set thee at liberty."

"Open the vessel," begged the genie. "Give me my liberty, and I promise to satisfy thee to thy own content."

"Thou art a traitor," replied the fisherman. "I should deserve to lose my life if I were such a fool as to trust thee."

"Hear me one word more," cried the genie; "I promise to do thee no hurt; nay, I will show thee a way to become exceedingly rich."

The hope of delivering himself from poverty prevailed with the fisherman. "I could listen to thee," said he, "were there any credit to be given to thy word. Swear to me by the great name of

God that you will faithfully perform what you promise, and I will open the vessel. I do not believe you will dare to break such an oath."

The genie swore to him, upon which the fisherman immediately took off the covering of the vessel, and at once the smoke ascended, and the genie having resumed his form, kicked the vessel into the sea.

"Be not afraid, fisherman," said the genie; "I only did it to see if thou wouldst be alarmed. To convince thee that I am in earnest, take thy nets and follow me."

They passed by the town and came to the top of a mountain, whence they descended into a vast plain, where lay a lake in the midst of four hills.

When they reached the side of the lake, the genie said to the fisherman, "Cast in thy nets, and catch fish."

The fisherman did not doubt of taking some, because he saw a great number in the water; but he was extremely surprised when he found they were of four colors, white, red, blue, and yellow. He threw in his nets and brought out one of each color. Having never seen the like before, he could not but admire them and, judging that he might get a considerable sum for them, he was very joyful.

"Carry those fish," said the genie to him, "and present them to thy sultan. He will give thee more money for them. Thou mayest come every day to fish in this lake; but I give thee warning not to throw in thy nets above once a day, otherwise thou wilt repent."

Having spoken thus, he struck his foot upon the ground, which opened, and after it had swallowed him up, closed again.

The Further
Adventures of the
Fisherman

THE fisherman being resolved to follow the genie's advice, forebore casting in his nets a second time and returned to the town very well satisfied. He went immediately to the sultan's palace to offer his fish.

The sultan was much surprised when he saw the four fish which the fisherman presented. He took them up one after another and viewed them with attention. "Take those fish," said he to his vizier, "and carry them to the cook—I cannot imagine but that they must be as good as they are beautiful—and give the fisherman four hundred pieces of gold."

The fisherman, who had never seen so much money, could scarcely believe his good fortune. He thought the whole must be a dream until he found it otherwise by being able to provide necessaries for his family.

As soon as the cook had cleaned the fish, she put them upon the fire in a frying pan, with oil, and when she thought them fried enough on one side, she turned them upon the other; but, O monstrous prodigy! scarcely were they turned, when the wall of the kitchen divided, and a young lady of wonderful beauty entered from the opening. She was clad in flowered satin, with pendants in her ears, a necklace of large pearls, and bracelets of gold set with rubies. A rod was in her hand.

She moved towards the frying pan, to the great amazement of the cook who continued fixed by the sight, and striking one of the fish with the end of the rod, said, "Fish, fish, are you on duty?"

The fish having answered nothing, she repeated these words, and then the four fish lifted up their heads and replied, "Yes, yes: if you reckon, we reckon; if you pay your debts, we pay ours; if you fly, we conquer and are content."

As soon as they had finished these words, the lady overturned the frying pan, and returned into the open part of the wall, which closed immediately and became as it was before.

The cook was greatly frightened at what had happened, but, coming a little to herself, went

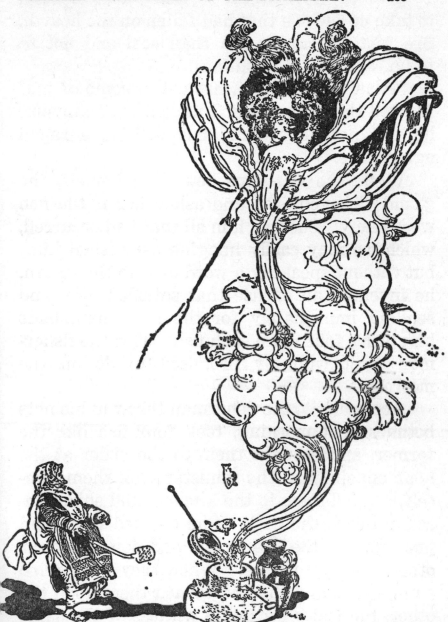

To the great amazement of the cook.

to take up the fish that had fallen on the hearth. She found them blacker than coal and not fit to be carried to the sultan.

"Alas!" said she, "what will become of me? If I tell the sultan what I have seen, I am sure he will not believe me but will be enraged against me."

While she was thus bewailing herself, the grand vizier entered and asked her if the fish were ready. She told him all that had occurred, which we may easily imagine astonished him; but without speaking a word of it to the sultan, he invented an excuse that satisfied him, and sending immediately for the fisherman, bade him bring four more such fish. This the fisherman most willingly promised to do on the morrow.

Accordingly, the fisherman threw in his nets betimes next morning, took four fish like the former, and brought them to the vizier at the hour appointed. The minister took them himself, carried them to the kitchen, and shut himself up with the cook. She cleaned them and put them on the fire as she had done the four others the day before. When they were fried on one side, and she had turned them upon the other, the vizier became a witness of the same events as the cook had narrated to him.

"This is too wonderful and extraordinary," said he, "to be concealed from the sultan. I will inform him of this prodigy."

The sultan, being much surprised, sent immediately for the fisherman and said to him, "Friend, can you bring me four more such fish?"

The fisherman replied, "If your majesty will be pleased to allow me until tomorrow, I will do it."

He caught four fish and brought them to the sultan who was so much rejoiced that he gave the fisherman four hundred pieces of gold. The sultan had the fish carried into his closet with all that was necessary for frying them. Having shut himself up with the vizier, the minister put them into the pan, and when they were fried on one side, turned them upon the other. Then the wall of the closet opened but, instead of the young lady, there came out a black, in the habit of a slave and of a gigantic stature, with a great green staff in his hand. He advanced towards the pan and, touching one of the fish with his staff, said with a terrible voice, "Fish are you on duty?"

At these words, the fish raised up their heads and answered, "Yes, yes, we are: if you reckon, we reckon; if you pay your debts, we pay ours; if you fly, we conquer and are content."

The fish had no sooner finished these words, than the black threw the pan into the middle of the closet and reduced the fish to a coal. Having done this, he retired fiercely and entered again into the aperture. It closed, and the wall appeared just as it did before.

The sultan sent for the fisherman, and on hearing where the fish had been caught, he commanded all his court to take horse, and the fisherman served them for a guide. They all ascended the mountain and at the foot of it they saw, to their great surprise, a vast plain that nobody had observed till then, and at last they came to the lake.

The sultan stood upon the bank, beholding the fish with admiration. On his demanding of his courtiers if it were possible they had never seen this lake, which was within so short a distance of the town, they all answered that they had never so much as heard of it.

"Since you all agree that you never heard of it, and as I am no less astonished than you are at this novelty, I am resolved not to return to my palace till I learn how this lake came here and why all the fish in it are of four colors." Having spoken thus, he ordered his court to encamp; and his pavilion and the tents of his household were planted upon the banks of the lake.

Resolved to withdraw alone from the camp to discover the secret of the portents that so disturbed his mind, the sultan bade his grand vizier inform the court that illness accounted for his absence until such time as he should return.

The grand vizier endeavored to divert the sultan from his design, but all to no purpose. The sultan was resolved. He put on a suit fit for walking and took his scimitar; and as soon as he found that all was quiet in the camp, went out alone. As the sun arose, he saw before him, at a considerable distance, a vast building of black polished marble, covered with fine steel, as smooth as glass. Being highly pleased that he had so speedily met with something worthy of his curiosity, he advanced towards the gate, which was partially open. Though he might immediately have entered, yet he thought it best to knock. This he did again and again, but as no one appeared, he was exceedingly surprised.

At last he entered, and when he came within the porch, he cried, "Is there no one here to receive a stranger who comes in for some refreshment as he passes by?" But though he spoke very loud, he was not answered. The silence increased his astonishment. He came into a spacious court and looked on every side for inhabitants, but discovered none.

He then entered several grand halls which were hung with silk tapestry, the alcoves and sofas being covered with stuffs of Mecca, and the porches with the richest stuffs of India, mixed with gold and silver.

Being tired with walking, he sat down on a veranda which had a view over the garden. Suddenly he heard the voice of one complaining in lamentable tones. He listened with attention and heard these words: "O fortune! thou hast not suffered me long to enjoy a happy lot! Forbear to persecute me, and by a speedy death put an end to my sorrows."

The sultan rose up, advanced towards the place whence came the voice, and opening the door of a great hall, pushed aside a curtain. A handsome young man, richly habited, was seated upon a throne. His face was sorrowful. The sultan drew near and saluted him.

The young man returned the salutation by an inclination of his head, at the same time saying, "My lord, I should rise to receive you; but I am hindered by sad necessity, and therefore I hope you will not be offended."

"My lord," replied the sultan, "I feel highly honored by your good opinion of me. As to the reason of your not rising, whatever your apology be, I heartily accept it. Being drawn hither by

A handsome young man, richly habited, was seated upon a throne.

your complaints, I come to offer you my help. But inform me the meaning of the lake near the palace, where the fish are of four colors; whose this castle is; how you came to be here; and why you are alone."

Instead of answering these questions, the young man began to weep bitterly. "How inconstant is fortune!" cried he. "She takes pleasure to pull down those she has raised." At these words, lifting up his robe, he showed the sultan that he was a man only from the head to the girdle and that the other half of his body was black marble.

You may easily imagine that the sultan was amazed when he saw the deplorable condition of the young man. "That which you show me," said he, "fills me with horror. I am impatient to hear your history, and I am persuaded that the lake and the fish make some part of it. Therefore I conjure you to relate it."

"I will not refuse your request," replied the young man, "though I cannot comply without renewing my grief." Thereupon he narrated the story of the young king of the Black Isles:

M Y FATHER, named Mahmoud, was king
of this country. This is the kingdom
of the Black Isles, which takes its name from
the four small neighboring mountains. Those
mountains were formerly isles. The capital was
on the spot now occupied by the lake you have
seen.

The king, my father, died when he was sev-
enty years of age; I had no sooner succeeded
him than I married my cousin. At first nothing
could surpass the harmony and pleasure of our
union. This lasted five years, at the end of
which time I perceived she ceased to delight in
my attentions.

One day, after dinner, while she was at the
bath, I lay down upon a sofa. Two of her ladies
came and sat down, one at my head and the

other at my feet, with fans in their hands to moderate the heat and to prevent the flies from disturbing me. They thought I was asleep, and spoke in whispers; but as I only closed my eyes, I heard all their conversation.

One of them said to the other, "Is not the queen wrong not to love so amiable a prince?"

"Certainly," replied the other; "I do not understand the reason, neither can I perceive why she goes out every night and leaves him alone. Is it possible that he does not perceive it?"

"Alas," said the first, "how should he? She mixes every evening in his liquor the juice of a certain herb which makes him sleep so sound all night that she has time to go where she pleases. As day begins to appear, she comes and lies down by him again and wakes him by the smell of something she puts under his nostrils."

You may guess, my lord, how much I was surprised at this conversation. I had, however, self-control enough to pretend to awake without having heard a word.

The queen returned from the bath, we supped together, and she presented me with a cup full of such water as I was accustomed to drink. Instead of putting it to my mouth, I went to a window that was open, threw out the water

They thought I was asleep, and spoke in whispers.

so quickly that she did not perceive it, and returned.

Soon after, believing that I was asleep, she
said, loud enough for me to hear her distinctly,
"Sleep on, and may you never wake again!" So
saying, she dressed herself and went out of the
chamber.

No sooner was she gone than I dressed myself in haste, took my scimitar, and followed her
so quickly that I soon heard the sound of her
feet before me, and then walked softly after her,
for fear of being heard. She passed through
several gates, which opened upon her pronouncing some magical words, and the last she opened
was that of the garden, which she entered. I
stopped at this gate, that she might not perceive
me, as she passed along a parterre; then looking
after her as far as the darkness of the night
permitted, I saw her enter a little wood. I went
thither by another way and, concealing myself,
saw her walking there with a man.

I did not fail to lend the most attentive ear
to their discourse, and heard her offer to fly to
another land with the fellow.

As the queen finished speaking, she and her
lover turned and passed before me. I had already drawn my scimitar, and her lover being
next me, I struck him to the ground. I con-

I concluded I had killed him.

cluded I had killed him, and therefore retired speedily without making myself known to the queen.

The wound I had given her lover was mortal, but by her enchantments she preserved him in an existence in which he could not be said to be either dead or alive. As I crossed the garden to return to the palace, I heard the queen loudly lamenting, and judging by her cries how much she was grieved, I was pleased that I had spared her life.

As soon as I had reached my apartment, I went to bed, and being satisfied with having punished the villain who had injured me, fell

asleep. When I awoke next morning, I found
the queen clad in mourning, her hair dishevelled.
"I come to beg your majesty not to be surprised
to see me in this condition," she said. "My heavy
affliction is occasioned by intelligence of three
distressing events—the death of the queen, my
dear mother; that of the king, my father, killed
in a battle; and of one of my brothers, who has
fallen down a precipice."

"Madam," said I, "so far from blaming, I
assure you I heartily commiserate your sorrow." I merely therefore expressed the hope
that time and reflection would moderate her
grief.

She begged permission to erect a burying
place for herself within the bounds of the palace,
where she would continue, she told me, to the
end of her days. I consented, and she built a
stately edifice and called it the Palace of Tears.
When it was finished, she caused her lover to be
conveyed thither. She had hitherto prevented
his dying by potions which she had administered
to him, and she continued to convey them to him
herself every day after he came to the Palace
of Tears.

Yet, with all her enchantments, she could
not cure him. He was not only unable to walk
or support himself, but had also lost the use of

his speech, and exhibited no sign of life except in his looks.

One day, my curiosity inducing me to go to the Palace of Tears, I heard her thus address her lover: "I am afflicted to the highest degree to behold you in this condition. Dear soul, I am continually speaking to you, and you do not answer me. How long will you remain silent? O tomb! hast thou destroyed that excess of affection which he bare me? Hast thou closed those eyes that evinced so much love?"

I must confess, my lord, I was enraged at these expressions and, in my turn, I cried, "O tomb! why dost not thou swallow up that monster so revolting to human nature?"

I had scarcely uttered these words, when the queen rose up like a fury. "Miscreant!" said she, "thou art the cause of my grief. By virtue of my enchantments, I command thee to become half marble and half man."

Immediately, my lord, I became what you see: a dead man among the living, and a living man among the dead.

After this cruel sorceress, unworthy of the name of queen, had metamorphosed me thus and brought me into this hall, by another enchantment she destroyed my capital, which was very flourishing and populous. She annihilated the houses, the public places, and markets. She reduced the site of the whole to the lake and desert plain you have seen. The fishes of four colors in the lake are the inhabitants of the four different religions which the city contained. The white are the Mussulmans; the red, the Persians, who worship fire; the blue, the Christians; and the yellow, the Jews. The four little hills were the four islands that gave name to this kingdom.

But this is not all. She comes every day and gives me over my naked shoulders a hundred lashes with a whip until I am covered with blood. When she has finished this part of my punishment, she throws over me a coarse stuff of goat's hair, and over that this robe of brocade to mock me.

The prince ended his story, and for a long time there was silence. Then the sultan, filled with anger, bade the young man tell him where the sorceress might be found that he might slay her. "Where is this Palace of Tears?" he demanded.

"It is on the side of the castle in which the gate is placed," answered the prince. "Every day at sunrise the queen goes thither."

"Then thither will I go and take vengeance upon the woman," cried the sultan.

They talked far into the night, and at dawn the sultan arose and proceeded to the Palace of Tears. He found it lighted with an infinite number of wax torches, and perfumed by a delicious scent issuing from several censers of fine gold.

As soon as he saw the senseless form of the lover on the couch, he drew his scimitar, destroyed the little remains of life left, and, dragging the body into the outer court, threw it into an unused well. After this, he went and lay down on the couch, placed his scimitar under the covering, and waited to complete his design.

The queen arrived shortly after in the chamber of her husband, the king of the Black Isles. In spite of his entreaties, she stripped him and gave him a hundred stripes. Then she put on again his covering of goat's hair and his robe of brocade.

She next went to the Palace of Tears and on entering began to renew her lamentations. "Alas," cried she, addressing herself to the sultan whom she supposed to be her lover, "wilt thou, light of my life, always preserve this silence?"

The sultan, lowering his voice as if in great weakness, spoke a few words.

Overjoyed, the sorceress gave a violent scream. "My dear lord," she exclaimed, "is it really you who speak to me?"

"Cruel woman," said the sultan, "art thou worthy of an answer?"

"Ah, do not reproach me," begged the queen.

The sultan continued in a low voice: "The cries, the groans and tears of your husband, whom you every day beat with such cruelty, prevent my rest. Make haste to set him at liberty that I be no longer disturbed by his lamentations."

The enchantress went immediately out of the Palace of Tears to fulfill these commands and, by the exercise of her spells, soon restored to the young king his natural shape, bidding him, however, on pain of death, to be gone from her presence instantly. The young king, yielding to necessity, retired to a remote place, where he patiently awaited the event of the design which the sultan had so happily begun. Meanwhile, the enchantress returned to the Palace of Tears and, supposing that she still spoke to her lover, assured him his behest had been obeyed.

The sultan, still disguising his voice, said: "What you have now done is by no means sufficient for my cure; bethink thee of the town, the islands, and the inhabitants destroyed by thy fatal enchantments. The fish every night at midnight raise their heads out of the lake and cry for vengeance against thee and me. This is the true cause of the delay of my cure. Go speedily, restore things to their former state, and at thy return I will give thee my hand, and thou shalt help me to arise."

The enchantress, inspired with hope, lost no time. She betook herself in all haste to the brink of the lake, where she took a little water in her hand and, sprinkling it, pronounced some word over the fish, whereupon the city was immediately restored. The fish became men, women, and children; Mohammedans, Christians, Persians, or Jews; freemen or slaves, as they were before—every one having recovered his natural form. The houses and shops were immediately filled with their inhabitants, who found all things as they were before the enchantment. The sultan's officers and attendants, who found themselves encamped in the largest square, were astonished to see themselves in an instant in the middle of a large, handsome, well-peopled city.

To return to the enchantress. As soon as she had effected this wonderful change, she returned with all expedition to the Palace of Tears, that she might receive her reward. "Come near," said the sultan. She did so. "You are not near enough. Nearer." She obeyed. He then rose up, and seizing her by the arm so suddenly that she had not time to discover him, he with a blow of his scimitar cut her in two, so that one half fell one way and the other another.

This done, he left the body on the spot and, going out of the Palace of Tears, went to seek the young king of the Black Isles. "Prince," said he, embracing him, "rejoice. You have now nothing to fear. Your cruel enemy is dead. You may henceforward dwell peaceably in your capital, unless you will accompany me to mine, which is not above four or five hours' journey distant."

"Potent monarch," replied the prince, "I do indeed believe that you came hither from your capital in the time you mention, because mine was enchanted; but since the enchantment is taken off, things are changed. It will take you no less than a year to return. However, this shall not prevent my following you, were it to the utmost corners of the earth."

The sultan was extremely surprised to understand that he was so far from his dominions, and could not imagine how it could be. "But," said he, "it is no matter; the trouble of returning to my own country is recompensed by acquiring you for a son; for since you will do me the honor to accompany me, I will make you my heir and successor."

At length, the sultan and the young prince began their journey, with a hundred camels laden with inestimable riches from the treasury of the young king, followed by fifty handsome men on horseback, perfectly well mounted and dressed. The inhabitants came out in great crowds, received him with joy, and made public rejoicings for several days.

The day after his arrival the sultan gave all his courtiers a complete account of the circumstances which had detained him so long. He informed them that he had adopted the king of the Four Black Isles, who was willing to leave a great kingdom to accompany and live with him; and, in reward for their loyalty, he made each of them presents according to their rank.

As for the fisherman, the sultan gave him a plentiful fortune, which made him and his family happy the rest of his days.

THERE was once a sultan of India who had three sons and one niece, the ornaments of his court. The eldest of the princes was called Houssain, the second Ali, the youngest Ahmed; and the princess, his niece, Nouronnihar.

The Princess Nouronnihar, having lost her father while she was still very young, had been brought up by the sultan. Now that she was grown to womanhood, the sultan thought of marrying her to some prince worthy of the alliance. She was very beautiful, and when the sultan's idea became known, the princes informed him, singly, that they loved her and would fain marry her.

This discovery pained the sultan, because he knew that there would be jealousy among his

He knew that there would be jealousy among his sons.

sons. He therefore sent for each separately
and spoke with him, urging him to abide per-
manently by the lady's choice, but none of them
would yield without a struggle. As he found
them obstinate, he sent for them all together,
and said:

"My children, since I have not been able to
dissuade you from aspiring to marry the princess, your cousin; and as I have no inclination
to use my authority to give her to one in preference to his brothers, I trust I have thought of an

expedient which will please you all and preserve harmony among you, if you will but hear me, and follow my advice. I think it would not be amiss if you were to travel separately into different countries, so that you might not meet each other; and, as you know I am very curious and delight in everything that is rare and singular, I promise my niece in marriage to him who shall bring me the most extraordinary rarity."

The three princes, each hoping that fortune would be favorable to him, consented to this proposal. The sultan gave them money; and early the next morning they started from the city, disguised as merchants. They departed by the same gate, each attended by a trusty servant, and for one day they journeyed together. They then halted at a khan* and, having agreed to meet in one year's time at the same place, they said farewell and, early the next morning, started on their several journeys.

Prince Houssain, the eldest brother, who had heard wonders of the extent, power, riches, and splendor of the kingdom of Bisnagar, bent his course towards the Indian coast. After three months' traveling, sometimes over deserts and barren mountains and sometimes through populous, fertile countries, he arrived at Bisnagar,

* Khan, an Oriental inn.

the capital of the kingdom of that name and the residence of its Maharajah. He lodged at a khan appointed for foreign merchants, and learned that there were four principal divisions where merchants of all sorts kept their shops. In the midst of these stood the Maharajah's palace, surrounded by three courts, and each gate distant two leagues from the other. He went to one of these quarters the next day.

Prince Houssain marveled at the variety and richness of the articles exposed for sale. As he wandered from street to street he wondered still more, for on all sides he saw the products of every country in the world. Silks, porcelain, and precious stones in abundance indicated the enormous wealth of the people.

Prince Houssain had finished his inspection, when a merchant, perceiving him passing with weary steps, asked him to sit down in his shop. Before long a crier came past, carrying a piece of carpet for which he asked forty purses of gold. It was only about six feet square, and the prince was astonished at the price. "Surely," said he, "there must be something very extraordinary about this carpet, which I cannot see, for it looks poor enough."

"You have guessed right, sir," replied the crier, "and will believe it when you learn that

A carpet for which he asked forty purses of gold.

whoever sits on this piece of carpeting may be transported in an instant whithersoever he desires to be, without being stopped by any obstacle."

The prince was overjoyed, for he had found a rarity which would secure the hand of the princess. "If," said he, "the carpet has this virtue, I will gladly buy it."

"Sir," replied the crier, "I have told you the truth, and it will be an easy matter to convince you. I will spread the carpeting; and when we have both sat down, and you have formed the wish to be transported into your apartment at the khan, if we are not conveyed thither, it shall be no bargain."

On this assurance of the crier, the prince accepted the conditions, and concluded the bargain. Having obtained the master's leave, they went into his back shop where they both sat down on the carpeting. As soon as the prince had formed his wish to be transported into his apartment at the khan, he in an instant found himself and the crier there. As he wanted not a more convincing proof of the virtue of the carpeting, he counted to the crier forty purses of gold, and gave him twenty pieces for himself.

For a time Prince Houssain tarried in the city, studying the manners and customs of the

people. He gained much satisfaction and information from visiting the different buildings and
witnessing the various ceremonies which took
place. But he desired to be nearer to the Prin-
eess Nouronnihar whom he most ardently loved,
and he considered that he could rely upon claiming her as his bride. Therefore, he paid his reck-
oning at the khan, spread the carpet upon the
floor of his room, and he and his attendant were
instantly transported to the meeting place from
which he had set out.

Prince Ali, the second brother, joined a caravan. In four months he arrived at Shiraz, which
was then the capital of the empire of Persia and,
having in the way contracted a friendship with
some merchants, passed for a jeweler and lodged
in the same khan with them.

On the morning after his arrival, Prince Ali
started to inspect the valuable articles which
were exposed for sale in the quarter where the
jewelers lodged. He was astonished by all the
wealth which he saw and he wandered from
street to street, lost in admiration. But what
surprised him most was a crier who walked to
and fro carrying an ivory tube in his hand, for
which he asked forty purses of gold. Prince Ali
thought the man mad, but he was anxious to
find out why the tube was so expensive. "Sir,"

The crier presented the tube for his inspection.

said the crier, when the prince addressed him, "this tube is furnished with a glass. By looking through it, you will see whatever object you wish to behold."

The crier presented the tube for his inspection; and he, wishing to see his father, looked through it and beheld the sultan in perfect health, sitting on his throne in his council chamber. Next he wished to see the Princess Nouronnihar, and immediately he saw her, sitting laughing among her companions.

Prince Ali wanted no other proof. He said to the crier, "I will purchase this tube from you for the forty purses." He then took him to the khan where he lodged, paid him the money, and received the tube.

Prince Ali was overjoyed at his purchase. He persuaded himself that, as his brothers would not be able to meet with anything so rare and admirable, the Princess Nouronnihar must become his bride. When all was ready, he joined his friends and arrived at the meeting place, where he found Prince Houssain, and both waited for Prince Ahmed.

Prince Ahmed took the road of Samarcand, and the day after his arrival, as he went through the city, he saw a crier who had an artificial apple in his hand for which he asked forty

It cures all sick persons.

purses of gold. "Let me see that apple," said
the prince, "and tell me what virtue or extraordinary property it possesses to be valued at
so high a rate."

"Sir," replied the crier, giving it into his
hand, "if you look at the mere outside of this
apple, it is not very remarkable; but if you consider its properties and the great use and benefit it is to mankind, you will say it is invaluable
and that he who possesses it is master of a great
treasure. It cures all sick persons of the most

mortal diseases; and this merely by the patient's smelling it."

"If one may believe you," replied Prince Ahmed, "the virtues of this apple are wonderful, and it is indeed valuable; but what proof have you of what you say?"

"Sir," replied the crier, "the truth is known to the whole city of Samarcand."

While the crier was detailing to Prince Ahmed the virtues of the artificial apple, many persons came about them and confirmed what he declared. One amongst the rest said he had a friend dangerously ill, whose life was despaired of, which was a favorable opportunity to show the experiment, upon which Prince Ahmed told the crier he would give him forty purses for the apple if it cured the sick person by smelling it.

The crier said to Prince Ahmed, "Come, sir, let us go and make the experiment, and the apple shall be yours."

The experiment succeeded; and the prince, after he had counted out to the crier forty purses, and had received the apple from him, waited with the greatest impatience for the departure of a caravan for the Indies.

When Prince Ahmed joined his brothers, they embraced with tenderness, and expressed much joy at meeting again. Then Prince Houssain said: "Brothers, let us postpone the narrative of our travels and let us at once show one another what we have bought as a curiosity that we may do ourselves justice beforehand, and judge to which of us our father may give the preference. To set the example, I will tell you that the rarity which I have brought from the kingdom of Bisnagar is the carpeting on which I sit. It looks but ordinary and makes no show, but it possesses wonderful virtues. Whoever sits on it and desires to be transported to any place is immediately carried thither. I made the experiment myself before I paid the forty purses which I most readily gave for it. I expect now that you should tell me whether what you have brought is to be compared with this carpet."

Prince Ali spoke next and said: "I must own that your carpet is very wonderful, yet I am as well satisfied with my purchase as you can possibly be with yours. Here is an ivory tube which also cost me forty purses. It looks ordinary enough, yet on looking through it you can behold whatever you desire to see, no matter how far distant it may be. Take it, brother, and try for yourself."

Houssain took the ivory tube from Prince Ali, with an intention to see the Princess Nouron-

nihar. Ali and Prince Ahmed, who kept their
eyes fixed upon him, were extremely surprised
to see his countenance change in such a manner
as expressed extraordinary alarm and affliction.
He cried out, "Alas! princes, to what purpose
have we undertaken such long and fatiguing
journeys with but the hope of being recompensed by the possession of the charming Nouronnihar, when in a few moments that lovely
princess will breathe her last. I saw her in her
bed surrounded by her women all in tears, who
seem to expect her death. Take the tube, behold
yourselves the miserable state she is in, and
mingle your tears with mine."

Prince Ali took the tube out of Houssain's
hand and, after he had seen the same object,
with sensible grief presented it to Ahmed, who
took it to behold the melancholy sight which so
much concerned them all.

When Prince Ahmed had taken the tube out
of Ali's hands, and saw that the Princess Nouronnihar's end was so near, he addressed himself to his two brothers and said, "Brothers, the
Princess Nouronnihar is indeed at death's door;
but, provided we lose no time, we may preserve
her life." He then took the artificial apple out
of his bosom and resumed, "This apple cost me
as much as the carpet or tube, and has healing

properties. If a sick person smells it, though in the last agonies, it will restore him to perfect health immediately. I have made the experiment and can show you its wonderful effect on the person of the Princess Nouronnihar, if we hasten to assist her."

"We cannot make more dispatch," said Prince Houssain, "than by transporting ourselves instantly into her chamber by means of my carpet. Come, lose no time. Sit down, it is large enough to hold us all."

Ali and Ahmed sat down by Houssain, and as their interest was the same, they all framed the same wish and were transported instantaneously into the Princess Nouronnihar's chamber.

The presence of three princes, who were so little expected, alarmed the princess's women who could not comprehend by what enchantment three men should be among them—for they did not know them at first.

Prince Ahmed no sooner saw himself in Nouronnihar's chamber, and perceived the princess dying, than he rose off the carpet and went to the bedside and put the apple to her nostrils. The princess instantly opened her eyes, and asked to be dressed, with the same freedom and recollection as if she had awaked out of a sound sleep. Her women presently informed her that she was obliged to the three princes, her cousins, and particularly to Prince Ahmed, for the sudden recovery of her health. She immediately expressed her joy at seeing them and thanked them all together, but afterwards Prince Ahmed in particular.

While the princess was dressing, the princes went to throw themselves at their father's feet. When they came to him, they found he had been previously informed of their unexpected arrival and by what means the princess had been so suddenly cured. The sultan received and embraced them with the greatest joy, both for their return and the wonderful recovery of the princess, his niece, who had been given over by the physicians.

After the usual compliments, each of the princes presented the rarity which he had brought: Prince Houssain his carpet, Prince Ali his ivory tube, and Prince Ahmed the artificial apple. After each had commended his present, as he put it into the sultan's hands, they begged of him to pronounce their fate and declare to which of them he would give the Princess Nouronnihar, according to his promise.

The sultan of the Indies having heard all that the princes had to say, remained some time

silent, considering what answer he should make.
At last he said to them in terms full of wisdom,
"I would declare for one of you, my children, if
I could do it with justice; but consider whether
I can? As for you, Houssain, the princess would
be very ungrateful if she did not show her sense
of the value of your carpet which was so necessary a means towards effecting her cure. But
consider, it would have been of little use if you
had not been acquainted with her illness by Ali's
tube or if Ahmed had not applied his artificial
apple. Therefore, as neither the carpet, the
ivory tube, nor the artificial apple has the least
preference to the other articles, I cannot grant
the princess to any one of you; and the only fruit
you have reaped from your travels is the glory
of having equally contributed to restore her to
health. As this is the case, you see that I must
have recourse to other means to determine the
choice I ought to make. As there is time
enough between this and night, I will do it today.
Go and procure each of you a bow and arrow,
repair to the plain where the horses are exer-
cised. I will soon join you and will give the
Princess Nouronnihar to him who shoots the
farthest."

The three princes had no objection to the decision of the sultan. When they were dismissed,

each provided himself with a bow and arrow,
and they went to the plain appointed, followed
by a great concourse of people.

The sultan did not make them wait long for
him. As soon as he arrived, Prince Houssain,
as the eldest, took his bow and arrow and shot
first. Prince Ali shot next, and much beyond
him; and Prince Ahmed last of all, but it so happened that nobody could see where his arrow
fell. Notwithstanding all the search made by
himself and all the spectators, it was not to be
found. Though it was believed that he had shot
the farthest, still, as his arrow could not be
found, the sultan determined in favor of Prince
Ali and gave orders for preparations to be made
for the solemnization of the nuptials, which were
celebrated a few days after with great magnifi-
cence.

Prince Houssain would not honor the feast
with his presence. He could not bear to see the
Princess Nouronnihar wed Prince Ali, who, he
said, did not deserve her better nor love her more
than himself. In short, his grief was so extreme
that he left the court. He renounced all right of
succession to the crown, turned dervish, and put
himself under the discipline of a famous sheik
who had gained great reputation for his ex-
emplary life.

He could not bear to see the Princess wed Prince Ali.

Prince Ahmed, urged by the same motive, did not attend the wedding; yet he did not renounce the world as Houssain had done. As he could not imagine what could have become of his arrow, he resolved to search for it that he might not have anything to reproach himself with. With this intent, he went to the place where Houssain's and Ali's arrows were gathered up and, proceeding straight-forwards from there, looked carefully on both sides as he advanced. He went so far that at last he began to think his labor was in vain; yet he could not help proceeding till he came to some steep craggy rocks, which completely barred the way.

To his great astonishment he perceived an arrow, which he recognized as his own, at the foot of the rocks. "Certainly," said he to himself, "neither I nor any man living could shoot an arrow so far. Perhaps fortune, to make amends for depriving me of what I thought the greatest happiness of my life, may have reserved a greater blessing for my comfort."

There were many cavities, into one of which the prince entered. Looking about, he beheld an iron door, which he feared was fastened; but, pushing against it, it opened, and disclosed an easy descent, which he walked down with his arrow in his hand. At first he thought he was going into a dark place, but presently a light quite different from that which he had quitted succeeded. He entered into a spacious square and beheld a magnificent palace. At the same instant, a lady of majestic air and of remarka-

"Come near, Prince Ahmed; you are welcome."

ble beauty, advanced. She was attended by a troop of ladies, all magnificently dressed.

As soon as Ahmed perceived the lady, he hastened to pay his respects; and the lady, seeing him, said, "Come near, Prince Ahmed. You are welcome."

Prince Ahmed was surprised at hearing himself addressed by name, but he bowed low, and followed into the great hall. Here she seated herself upon a sofa and requested the prince to sit beside her. Then she said: "You are surprised that I know you, yet you cannot be ignorant, as the Koran informs you, that the world is inhabited by genies as well as men. I am the daughter of one of the most powerful and distinguished of these genies. My name is Perie Banou. I am no stranger to your loves or your travels. It was I myself who exposed to sale the artificial apple which you bought at Samarcand, the carpet which Prince Houssain purchased at Bisnagar, and the tube which Prince Ali brought from Shiraz. You seemed to me worthy of a more happy fate than that of possessing the Princess Nouronnihar; and that you might attain to it, I carried your arrow to the place where you found it. It is in your power to avail yourself of the favorable opportunity which presents itself to make you happy."

Ahmed made no answer, but knelt to kiss the hem of her garment; but she would not allow him, and presented her hand, which he kissed a thousand times and kept fast locked in his.

"Well, Prince Ahmed," said she, "will you pledge your faith to me, as I do mine to you?"

"Yes, madam," replied the prince in an ecstasy of joy. "What can I do more fortunate for myself, or with greater pleasure?"

"Then," answered the fairy, "you are my husband, and I am your wife. Our fairy marriages are contracted with no other ceremonies, and yet are more indissoluble than those among men with all their formalities."

The fairy Perie Banou then conducted Prince Ahmed round the palace, where he saw much that delighted him, and showed the wealth of the palace. At last she led him to a rich apartment in which the marriage feast was spread. The fairy had ordered a sumptuous repast to be prepared; and the prince marveled at the variety and delicacy of the dishes, many of which were quite strange to him. While they ate there was music, and after dessert, a large number of fairies and genies appeared and danced before them.

Day after day new amusements were provided, each more entrancing than the last, and every day he grew more and more in love with the beautiful Perie Banou.

At the end of six months he bethought him of his father and asked permission to visit him, but the genie persuaded him not to go. "Only harm would come of it, my love," she told him.

Meantime his father, the Sultan of the Indies, grieved over the loss of his two sons. He had learned of Houssain and of his place of retreat, but there was no trace of Ahmed. He called to his aid a sorceress, but she was unable to find the missing prince.

As the days went by, Prince Ahmed did not renew his request for permission to visit his father; but the fairy, Perie Banou, saw that the desire was in his mind and at last said to him, "Prince, I can see you are grieving for a sight of your father and I am willing to let you go, but you must promise that your absence shall not be long. Do not speak of your marriage or of the place of our residence. Let your parent be satisfied with the knowledge that you are happy."

Prince Ahmed was greatly pleased at this. Accompanied by twenty horsemen, he set out on a charger which was most richly caparisoned and as beautiful a creature as any in the sultan of the Indies' stables. It was no great distance to his father's capital. When Prince Ahmed arrived, the people received him with acclamations and followed him in crowds to the palace. The sultan embraced him with great joy, complaining at the same time with a fatherly tenderness, of the affliction his long absence had occasioned.

"Sir," replied Prince Ahmed, "when my arrow so mysteriously disappeared, I wanted to find it; and returning alone, I commenced my search. I sought all about the place where Houssain's and Ali's arrows were found, and where I imagined mine must have fallen, but all my labor was in vain. I proceeded along the plain in a straight line for a league and found nothing. I

was about to give up my search, when I found
myself drawn forward against my will. After
having gone four leagues, to that part of the
plain where it is bounded by rocks, I saw an
arrow. I ran to the spot, took up the arrow, and
knew it to be the same which I had shot. Then
I knew that your decision was faulty, and that
some power was working for my good. But as
to this mystery, I beg you will not be offended
if I remain silent, and that you will be satisfied
to know that I am happy and content with my
fate. Nevertheless, I was grieved lest you
should suffer in uncertainty, and I beg you to
allow me to come here occasionally to visit
you."

"Son, I wish to penetrate no farther into your
secrets. Your presence has restored to me the
joy I have not felt for a long time, and you shall
always be welcome when you can come."

Prince Ahmed stayed three days at his
father's court and on the fourth returned to the
fairy, Perie Banou, who received him with great
joy.

Once every month Ahmed visited his father
and was received by the sultan with the same
joy and satisfaction. For several months he
constantly paid him visits, and always with a
richer and more brilliant equipage.

At last the sultan's favorites, who judged of Prince Ahmed's power by the splendor of his appearance, contrived to make him jealous of his son. He sent for the sorceress and bade her watch where his son went. The sorceress was more successful this time, following Ahmed to the beautiful palace and, by feigning sickness, had herself carried within. The fairy Perie Banou, taking pity on the woman, directed two of her ladies in waiting to conduct the sorceress to a splendid apartment. She was laid on a luxurious bed, and one of the attendants brought her a cup, full of a certain liquor. "Drink this," she said; "it is the water of the fountain of lions and a potent remedy against fevers. You will find the effect of it in less than an hour's time."

The attendants then left her and returned at the end of an hour. When she saw them open the door of the apartment, she cried out, "O the admirable potion! it has wrought its cure, and I have waited with impatience to desire you to conduct me to your charitable mistress, as I would not lose time but prosecute my journey."

The two women conducted her through several apartments, all more superb than that wherein she had lain, into a large hall, the most richly and magnificently furnished in all the palace.

Perie Banou was seated in this hall, upon a throne of massive gold, enriched with diamonds, rubies, and pearls of an extraordinary size, and attended on each hand by a great number of beautiful fairies, all richly dressed. At the sight of so much splendor, the sorceress was not only dazzled, but so struck that, after she had prostrated herself before the throne, she could not open her lips to thank the fairy as she had purposed. However, Perie Banou saved her the trouble, and said, "Good woman, I am glad that you are able to pursue your journey. I will not detain you, but perhaps you may like to see my palace. Follow my women, and they will show it to you."

The old sorceress, who had not power or courage to say a word, prostrated herself once more with her head on the carpet that covered the foot of the throne, took her leave, and was conducted by the two fairies through the palace. Afterwards they conducted her to the iron gate through which she had entered and let her depart, wishing her a good journey.

On her return the sorceress related to the sultan how she had succeeded in entering the fairy's palace and told him all the wonders she had seen there. When she had finished her narrative the sorceress said: "I shudder when I consider the misfortunes which may happen to you, for who can say that the fairy may not inspire him with the unnatural design of dethroning your majesty and seizing the crown of the Indies? This is what your majesty ought to consider as of the utmost importance."

The sultan of the Indies had been consulting with his favorites, when he was told of the sorceress's arrival. He now ordered her to follow him to them. He acquainted them with what he had learned might happen. Then one of the favorites said: "In order to prevent this, now that the prince is in your power, you ought to put him under arrest. I would not take away his life, but make him a close prisoner." This advice all the other favorites applauded.

But the sorceress said, "No. The fairy would work some spells on us if we imprisoned her husband. A better way is to make demands on his filial love, and if he refuses, then we will have just cause for complaint. For example, ask him to procure you a tent which can be carried in a man's hand but so large as to shelter your whole army."

The sultan agreed, and made this request to his son on his next visit.

"What! prince," cried she, "do you think I jest with you?"

Prince Ahmed was greatly embarrassed but said he would present the request to Perie Banou. He returned to the palace, shamefaced. To his surprise the fairy only laughed. "It is but a trifle," she told him. "I will gladly give your father what he desires."

She then sent for her treasurer to whom she said, "Noor-Jehaun, bring me the largest pavilion in my treasury."

Noor-Jehaun returned presently with a pavilion which could not only be held, but concealed, in the palm of the hand and presented it to her mistress, who gave it to Prince Ahmed to look at.

When Prince Ahmed saw the pavilion, which the fairy called the largest in her treasury, he fancied she had a mind to banter him, and his surprise soon appeared in his countenance. Perie Banou perceived it and laughed. "What! prince," cried she, "do you think I jest with you? You will see that I am in earnest. Noor-Jehaun," said she to her treasurer, "go and set it up, that he may judge whether the sultan will think it large enough."

The treasurer immediately took it from the palace and set it up. The prince found it large enough to shelter two armies as numerous as that of his father. "You see," said the fairy, "that the pavilion is larger than your father may have occasion for, but you are to observe that it has the property of becoming larger or smaller, according to the extent of the army it has to cover, without applying any hands to it."

The treasurer took down the tent again, reduced it to its first size, brought it and put it
into the prince's hands. He took it, and without
staying longer than till the next day, mounted
his horse and rode off to the sultan his father.

The sultan was in great surprise at the
prince's speedy return. He took the tent, but,
after he had admired its smallness, his amazement was so great that he could not recover
himself when he had it set up in the great plain
before mentioned and found it large enough to
shelter an army twice as large as he could bring
into the field.

The sultan expressed great obligation to the
prince for so noble a present, desiring him to
return his thanks to the fairy. To show what
a value he set upon it, he ordered it to be carefully laid up in his treasury. But within himself he felt greater jealousy than ever of his son.
Therefore, more intent upon his ruin, he went
to consult the sorceress again. She advised the
sultan to engage the prince to bring him some
of the water of the fountain of lions.

In the evening, when the sultan was surrounded as usual by all his court and the prince
came to pay his respects among the rest, he put
forward his request for a bottle of the curative
water.

Again Ahmed returned to the fairy Perie Banou and unwillingly tendered his father's second request.

"I do not ask this of myself," he said stammeringly. "I do but repeat the words of my father, the sultan; and I am grieved that he was not content with what you did for him before. I leave it to your own pleasure whether you will gratify or reject this new desire. It shall be as you please."

"No, no," replied the fairy, "I will satisfy him, and whatever advice the sorceress may give him (for I see that he hearkens to her counsel), he shall find no fault with you or me. There is much wickedness in this demand, as you will understand by what I am going to tell you. The fountain of lions is situated in the middle of a court of a great castle, the entrance into which is guarded by four fierce lions, two of which sleep alternately, while the other two are awake. But let not that frighten you. I will supply you with means to pass by them without danger."

The fairy Perie Banou was at work with her needle. She took one of several clues* of thread before her and, presenting it to Prince Ahmed, said, "First, take this clue of thread. I will tell you presently the use of it. In the second place,

---
*Clue, skein.

you must have two horses. One you must ride yourself, and the other you must lead. It will be loaded with a sheep, which must be killed today, cut into four quarters. In the third place, you must be provided with a bottle, which I will give you, to bring the water in. Set out early tomorrow morning, and when you have passed the iron gate, throw before you the clue of thread, which will roll till it reaches the gates of the castle. Follow it, and when it stops, as the gates will be open, you will see the four lions. The two that are awake will, by their roaring, wake the other two. Be not alarmed, but throw each of them a quarter of the sheep, and then clap spurs to your horse and ride to the fountain. Fill your bottle without alighting, and return with the same expedition. The lions will be so busy eating they will let you pass unmolested."

Prince Ahmed set out the next morning at the time appointed him by the fairy and followed her directions punctually. When he arrived at the gates of the castle, he distributed the quarters of the sheep among the four lions and, passing through the midst of them, reached the fountain, filled his bottle, and returned safely. When he had got a little distance from the castle gates, he turned about and, perceiving two of the lions coming after him, drew his sabre and prepared himself for defense. But as he went forward, he saw one of them turn out of the road at some distance and show by his head and tail that he did not come to do him any harm, but only to go before him, and that the other stayed behind to follow. He therefore put his sword again into its scabbard. Guarded in this manner, he arrived at the capital of the Indies. The lions never left him till they had conducted him to the gates of the sultan's palace, after which they returned the way they had come. Notwithstanding they walked gently and showed no signs of fierceness, the alarmed populace fled or hid themselves to avoid them.

A number of officers came to attend the prince while he dismounted and conduct him to the apartment of the sultan, who was at that time conversing with his favorites. He approached the throne, laid the bottle at the sultan's feet, kissed the carpet which covered the footstool, and rising, said, "I have brought you, sir, the salutary water which your majesty so much desired. At the same time I wish you such health as never to have occasion to make use of it."

After the prince had concluded, the sultan placed him on his right hand and said, "Son, I am much obliged to you for this valuable present; but I have one thing more to ask of you, after which I shall expect nothing more from your obedience, nor from your interest with your wife. This request is to bring me a man not above a foot and a half high, whose beard is thirty feet long, who carries upon his shoulders a bar of iron of five hundredweight, which he uses as a quarter-staff, and who can speak."

The next day the prince returned to Perie Banou, to whom he related his father's new demand, which, he said, he looked upon to be a thing more impossible than the two first. "For," added he, "I cannot imagine there is or can be such a man in the world."

"Do not alarm yourself, prince," replied the fairy. "You ran a risk in fetching the water of the fountain of lions for your father, but there is no danger in finding this man. It is my brother Schaibar, who is far from being like me, though we both had the same father. He is of so violent a nature that nothing can prevent his giving bloody marks of his resentment for a slight offence; yet, on the other hand, is so liberal as to oblige any one in whatever his desire. I will send for him, but prepare yourself not to be alarmed at his extraordinary figure."

"What! my queen," replied Prince Ahmed, "do you say Schaibar is your brother? Let him be ever so ugly or deformed, I shall love and honor him as my nearest relation."

The fairy ordered a gold chafing dish to be set with a fire in it under the porch of her palace. She took some incense and threw it into the fire whence there arose a thick cloud of smoke.

Some moments after, the fairy said to Prince Ahmed, "Prince, there comes my brother, do you see him?" The prince immediately perceived Schaibar, who looked at the prince with fierce eyes, and asked Perie Banou who that man was. To which she replied, "He is my husband, brother; his name is Ahmed; he is a son of the sultan of the Indies; on his account I have taken the liberty now to call for you."

At these words, Schaibar, looking at Prince Ahmed with a favorable eye, which however diminished neither his fierceness nor savage look, said, "It is enough for me that he is your husband. I will do for him whatever he desires."

"The sultan his father," replied Perie Banou, "is curious to see you, and I desire he may be your guide to the sultan's court."

"He needs but lead the way, I will follow him," replied Schaibar.

The next morning Schaibar set out with Prince Ahmed to visit the sultan. When they arrived at the gates of the capital, the people, as soon as they saw Schaibar, ran and hid themselves. Some fled to their shops and houses, shutting their doors, while others, taking to their heels, communicated their fear to all they met, who stayed not to look behind them. When Schaibar and Prince Ahmed, as they went along, found all the streets and squares desolate they came to the palace, the porters, instead of preventing Schaibar from entering, ran away too; so that the prince and he advanced without any obstacle to the council hall, where the sultan was seated on his throne, giving audience.

Schaibar went fiercely up to the throne, without waiting to be presented, and accosted the sultan in these words: "You have asked for me. Speak!"

The sultan turned away his head to avoid the sight of so terrible an object. Schaibar was so much provoked at this rude reception that he instantly lifted up his iron bar and let it fall on his head, killing him before Prince Ahmed could intercede in his behalf.

Schaibar then smote all the favorites who had given the sultan bad advice. He spared the grand vizier, who was a just man. When this

terrible execution was over, Schaibar came out
of the council hall into the courtyard with the
iron bar upon his shoulder and, looking at the
grand vizier, said, "I know there is here a certain sorceress who is a greater enemy of the
prince my brother-in-law than all those base
favorites I have chastised. Let her be brought
to me immediately."

The grand vizier instantly sent for her, and
as soon as she was brought, Schaibar slew her
with his iron bar.

"After this," he said, "I will treat the whole
city in the same manner if they do not immediately acknowledge Prince Ahmed, my brother-
in-law, as sultan of the Indies."

Then all who were present made the air ring
with repeated acclamations of "Long life to Sultan Ahmed!" Schaibar caused him to be clothed
in the royal vestments, installed him on the
throne, and after he had made all swear homage
and fidelity, returned to his sister Perie Banou,
whom he brought with great pomp and made
her sultana of the Indies.

Prince Ali and Princess Nouronnihar were
given a considerable province, with its capital,
where they spent the rest of their lives. Afterwards he sent an officer to Houssain to acquaint
him with the change and make him an offer of

any province he might choose. That prince thought himself so happy in his solitude that he desired the officer to return his brother thanks for the kindness he proposed, assuring him of his submission. He said that the only favor he desired was to be indulged with leave to retire to the palace he had chosen for his retreat.

The Story of
Aladdin, or the
Wonderful Lamp

ALADDIN was the son of a poor tailor, by name Mustapha, in one of the rich provinces of China. When he was old enough to learn a trade, his father took him into his own shop, but Aladdin was an idle fellow and loved play better than work.

His father died while Aladdin was yet very young. However he was as idle as before, and his mother was obliged to spin cotton night and day in order to support herself and him.

One day, when he was about fifteen years old, he was playing in the streets with some of his companions. Soon a stranger who was passing by stopped and looked at him. This stranger was a famous African magician who was in need of a helper. As soon as he saw Aladdin, he knew by his manner and appearance that he was well suited to his purpose. The magician then asked Aladdin's name of some persons standing near by.

He crowded in among the boys, placed his hand on Aladdin's shoulder, and said, "My good lad, are you not the son of Mustapha, the tailor?"

"Yes, sir," replied Aladdin, "but my father has been dead a long time."

"Alas!" cried the magician, "what sad news! I am your father's brother. I have been away for many years, and now when I have come home in the hope of seeing him, you tell me he is dead!" While tears ran down the stranger's cheeks, he pulled out a purse and gave Aladdin two pieces of gold. "Take these, my boy," he said, "and give them to your mother. Tell her that I will come and sup with her tonight."

Pleased with the money, Aladdin ran home to his mother. "Mother," said he, "have I an uncle?"

She told him he had not. Then Aladdin gave her the gold and told her that a man who said he was his father's brother was coming to sup with them that evening. The good woman was astonished, but she went to the market and bought provisions and was preparing the supper when the magician knocked at the door. He entered, followed by a porter who brought all kinds of delicious fruits and sweetmeats.

After the magician had given Aladdin the
things he had brought, he saluted his mother,
and asked to be shown the couch on which his
brother Mustapha had been in the habit of sitting. When this was done, he fell down and
kissed it several times. Then he said with tears
in his eyes, "My poor brother, how unhappy I
am because I did not come soon enough to give
you a last embrace!"

As soon as they sat down to supper, the magician gave Aladdin's mother an account of his
travels. He said he had been away from home
for forty years and had traveled to distant countries. Then he turned to Aladdin and asked his
name.

"I am called Aladdin," said he.

"Well, Aladdin," replied the magician, "what
business do you follow? Have you any trade?"

At these questions Aladdin hung his head
and was much ashamed. His mother replied,
"Aladdin is an idle fellow. His father tried to
teach him his trade, but he did not succeed.
Since his father's death, he has done nothing but
idle away his time in the streets."

With these words the poor woman burst into
tears, and the magician turned to Aladdin and
said, "This is not well, my nephew. You must
think of some way of earning a living. I will

help you in any way I can. Shall I take a shop
and furnish it for you?"

Aladdin was overjoyed at the idea, for he
thought there was very little work in keeping a
shop. He told his uncle this would suit him
better than anything else.

"I will take you with me tomorrow," said
the magician, "and clothe you as handsomely as
any merchant in the city. Then we will open
a shop."

Aladdin's mother thanked the magician very
heartily and begged Aladdin to behave so as to
prove himself worthy of the good fortune promised by his kind uncle.

Next day the stranger called for Aladdin as
he had promised, and led him to a merchant who
sold ready-made clothes. Then he had Aladdin
try on the handsomest suits and bought the one
that he liked best. The pretended uncle then
took Aladdin to visit the bazaars where the foreign merchants were, and gave him a feast.

When Aladdin's mother saw him return so
handsomely dressed and heard him tell of the
company he had been in, she was full of joy.
"Generous brother," said she to the magician,
"I do not know how to thank you enough for
your goodness. May you live many years and
have my son's gratitude!"

"Aladdin," replied he, "is a good boy. I have no doubt that some day we shall both be proud of him. I am sorry that I cannot hire the shop for Aladdin tomorrow, as it is Friday, and all the merchants will be absent, so I will come to take Aladdin and show him the public gardens outside the town."

The next morning Aladdin got up very early and dressed himself. Soon he saw his uncle coming, and ran to meet him. The magician greeted him very kindly and said, "Come, my good boy, today I will show you some very fine things."

Then he led him through beautiful gardens with great houses standing in them. By degrees he led him on farther and farther in the country. At last, seeing that Aladdin was tired, he bade him sit down by the side of a great basin of pure water. He also gave him some cakes and fruits, and told him to eat them.

By kindness and pleasant talk he led Aladdin to go much farther until they came to a narrow valley with mountains on all sides. This was the place that the magician had hoped to reach. He had brought Aladdin for a secret purpose of his own.

"We shall go no farther," said he to Aladdin. "I shall show you some wonders that no one

besides yourself will ever see. I am now going
to make a fire, so gather all the dry sticks and
leaves that you can find."

There were many dry sticks scattered about,
so that Aladdin soon gathered more than
enough. The magician lighted a fire and, as
soon as it was in a blaze, he threw some perfume
into it. A dense smoke rose and the magician
spoke some mysterious words. At the same instant the ground shook and opened near the spot
where they stood. They could see a square stone
about a foot and a half across, with a brass ring
fastened in the center of it.

Aladdin was frightened out of his wits and
was about to run away, when the magician suddenly gave him a blow on the ear and knocked
him down. Poor Aladdin trembled and, with
tears in his eyes, got up and said, "Dear uncle,
what have I done to deserve so severe a
blow?"

"I have good reasons for it," replied the magician. "Obey me, and you will not be sorry for
it. Underneath that stone is a treasure which
will make you richer than many kings if you will
do what I tell you to."

By this time Aladdin was over his fright and
said, "What must I do? Tell me. I am ready
to obey you."

"Well said," replied the magician. "Now come and take hold of this ring and lift up the stone."

To Aladdin's surprise, the stone was raised without any trouble, and then he could see a small opening three or four feet deep. At the bottom of this was a little door, with steps that led down still lower.

"Now," said the magician, "you must go down into this cavern. When you come to the bottom of the steps, you will see an open door leading into three great halls. In each of these you will see four vases as large as tubs, full of gold and silver, but you must take care not to touch any of it. When you come into the first hall, take up your robe and bind it around you. Then go on to the second hall and from there to the third.

"Above all, be very careful not to go near the walls nor even to touch them with your robe. If any part of your dress should chance to touch them, your instant death will be the result. At the end of the third hall, there is a door that leads to a garden full of beautiful trees covered with fruit. Go straight on and follow a path that you will see. This will lead you to the bottom of a flight of fifty steps, at the top of which there is a wall.

"When you reach the wall, you will see a shelf on which there is a lighted lamp. Take up the lamp and put out the light. Then throw away the wick and the oil and put the lamp in your bosom. Then bring it to me. If you should wish to gather any of the fruit in the garden, you may do so. There is nothing to prevent you from taking as much as you please."

When the magician had given these directions, he took a ring from one of his fingers and gave it to Aladdin, telling him that it would protect him from any evil.

"Now go, my child," said the magician. "We shall both be rich for the rest of our lives."

Aladdin leaped into the opening and went down to the bottom of the steps. He found the three halls exactly as the magician had said. He passed through them with the greatest care for fear of being killed. He went on to the garden and climbed to the wall. He took down the lamp, emptied it, and put it in his girdle.

Then he started back but stopped in the garden to look at the fruit. The trees were all full of the most wonderful fruit. Some were white and others sparkled like crystals. Some were red and some green, some blue and some violet. The white were pearls, the sparkling kinds were diamonds. The red were rubies, the green were emeralds, the blue were turquoises, and the violet, amethysts. In short, all the fruits were precious stones—and they were larger and more perfect than any that had ever been seen in the whole world.

Aladdin was not yet old enough to know their value, and thought they were all only colored glass. However, their beautiful colors pleased him and he gathered some of each color and filled both his pockets as well as the two new purses that the magician had bought for him.

Loaded down in this manner with the immense treasure, Aladdin hurried through the three halls, in order that he might not make the magician wait too long. Having passed through them with the same caution as before, he began to ascend the steps. Soon he reached the entrance of the cave, where the magician was waiting. As soon as Aladdin saw him he called out, "Give me your hand, uncle, and help me up."

"My dear boy," replied the magician, "first give me the lamp, so that will not hinder you."

"It is not at all in my way," said Aladdin, "and I will give it to you when I am out."

The magician still insisted on having the lamp before he helped Aladdin out of the cave; but the lamp was covered with the fruit from the trees, and the lad could not easily find it

until he got out of the cave. This threw the
magician into the most violent rage. He threw
a little perfume upon the fire, which he had kept
burning, and he had hardly pronounced two
magic words before the stone returned to its own
place and shut up the entrance of the cavern.

Aladdin did not expect such a wicked action
by his supposed uncle after all his kindness and
generosity. He was more horrified than can be
told. When he found himself buried alive, he
called a thousand times to his uncle, telling him
he would give him the lamp. But all his cries
were useless, and he remained there in darkness.

At last he dried his tears and went down to
the bottom of the stairs, intending to go into
the garden; but the walls, which had been opened
by enchantment, were now closed. He felt all
around him to the right and the left, but could
not find the least opening. Then he sat down
on the steps and redoubled his cries and tears.

Aladdin remained here for two days, without
eating or drinking. On the third day, feeling
that death was near, he clasped his hands in
prayer, and said in a loud voice, "There is no
power but in God."

As he joined his hands, he happened to rub
the ring which the magician had put upon his
finger.

As soon as it was rubbed, a genie of enormous size and terrible appearance rose out of the earth before him. "What do you wish?" said he to Aladdin. "I am ready to obey you as your slave. I am the slave of him who wears the ring on his finger."

Frightened almost out of his wits, Aladdin cried, "Whoever you are, take me out of this place!"

Scarcely had he said it, when he found himself on the outside of the cave, at the very spot where the magician had left him. He rose up trembling and made his way back to the city. When he reached his mother's door, he was fainting from hunger and fatigue.

His mother, who was heartbroken because he had not returned, received him joyfully and gave him food and drink. Then he told his mother all that had happened to him, and showed her the lamp and the colored fruits and the wonderful ring on his finger.

However, his mother thought little of the jewels, as she was ignorant of their value. Aladdin hid them behind the sofa, while his mother bewailed the wickedness of the magician.

When Aladdin awoke next morning, his first thought was that he was very hungry and would like some breakfast.

A genie of enormous size rose out of the earth.

"Alas, my child," replied his mother, "I have not a morsel of bread to give you. You ate last night the last bits of food in the house. However, I have a little cotton of my own spinning, and I will go and sell it and buy something for dinner."

"Keep your cotton, mother," replied Aladdin, "and give me the lamp that I brought with me yesterday. I will go and sell that, and the money I shall receive will buy us food for breakfast and dinner."

Aladdin's mother took the lamp from the shelf where she had put it. "Here it is," she said, "but it is very dirty. If I polish it a little, perhaps it will sell for more."

Then she took some water and a little sand to clean it with. But she had scarcely begun to rub this lamp, when instantly, and while her son was present, a horrible genie rose out of the ground before her and cried with a voice as loud as thunder, "What do you wish? I am ready to obey you as your slave. I am the slave of those who have the lamp in their hands."

Aladdin's mother was too terrified to speak, but Aladdin, who had seen a genie in the cavern, seized the lamp, and answered in a firm voice, "I am hungry. Bring me something to eat at once."

The genie disappeared, and returned in a moment. He carried on his head a silver tray on which were twelve silver dishes filled with the finest food. There were also six silver plates and two silver cups. He placed them all upon the table and instantly disappeared.

When Aladdin's mother had recovered from her fright, they both sat down to their breakfast in great delight. Never before had they eaten such delicious food or seen such fine dishes.

This feast provided them with food for several days, and when it was all gone, Aladdin sold the silver dishes one by one and bought more food. In this way they lived happily for a number of years, for Aladdin now behaved with great wisdom. He took care to visit the principal shops and public places, and in this way grew to be very wise.

One day, as he was walking in the city, Aladdin heard an order of the sultan, telling all persons to shut up their shops, and go into their houses until Princess Badroulbadour, the daughter of the sultan, had passed by on her way to the bath.

Aladdin hurried along with the crowd of people until he found himself in the doorway of a large building. He placed himself behind the door, where he was certain not to be

seen, and where he might see the princess
as she passed.

He had not long to wait before she came,
with a great crowd of her attendants. As she
passed, she threw aside her veil, so that Aladdin
saw her face. She was indeed the most beautiful princess he had ever seen, and he fell in love
with her at once.

When Aladdin told his mother of his love for
the princess, she laughed, and said, "Alas, my
son, what are you thinking of? You must have
lost your senses to talk so foolishly."

"Mother," replied Aladdin, "I have not lost
my senses; I am in my right mind. I knew very
well that you would think me a fool, but whatever you may say, nothing will prevent me from
asking the princess in marriage."

"Truly, my son," said his mother, "you seem
to have forgotten that your father was but a
poor tailor. Indeed, I do not know who will dare
to go and speak to the sultan about it."

"You must go yourself," said he.

"I?" cried his mother in great surprise. "I
go to the sultan? No, indeed, I will take care
not to do anything so foolish. You know very
well that no one can make any request of the
sultan without bringing a rich present, and
where shall such poor folk as we find a present?"

The luster of the gems . . . dazzled their eyes.

Then Aladdin told his mother that while talking with the merchants in the shops he had learned to know the value of something that they owned. For a long time he had known that nothing that they had in their shops was half so fine as those jewels he had brought home from the enchanted cave. So his mother brought them from the place where they had long been hidden. Together they arranged them in a fine porcelain dish. The brightness and luster of the gems, and the variety of the colors, so dazzled their eyes that they were astonished beyond measure.

Aladdin's mother was sure that her son's present was one that could not fail to please the sultan, so she agreed to do as her son wished. She took the porcelain dish with the jewels and folded it up in a very fine linen cloth. Then she set out and took the road to the palace of the sultan. The grand vizier, accompanied by the other viziers and proper officers of the court, had already gone in when she arrived at the gate. The crowd of those who had business at the court was very great. The doors were opened, and she went in with the others. She placed herself so that she was opposite the sultan and other officers.

After the various persons had been heard, the sultan and his court retired, without anyone taking the slightest notice of Aladdin's mother. Day after day the good woman went back, until at last her patience touched the sultan's heart. One day he sent for her and asked her what she wanted.

Trembling, Aladdin's mother told him of her son's request and begged the mercy of the sultan for him and for herself. The sultan heard her kindly, and then asked her what she had so care-

The grand vizier.

"I will wait till you bring me his answer."

fully tied up in the linen cloth. Then she **un-folded** the cloth, and laid the sparkling jewels before him. It is impossible to express the astonishment of the sultan when he saw the jewels in that dish.

For several moments he gazed at them speechless. Then he took the present from the hand of Aladdin's mother, and exclaimed, "How very beautiful! How very rich!"

"My good woman, I will indeed make your son happy by marrying him to the princess as soon as he shall send me forty large basins of gold full of the same kind of jewels that you have already presented to me. They must be brought

to me by an equal number of black slaves, each
of whom shall be led by a white slave, all richly
dressed. Go, now, my good woman, and I will
wait till you bring me his answer."

Full of disappointment, Aladdin's mother
made her way home, and told her son the sultan's strange wish. But Aladdin only smiled,
and when his mother had gone out, he took the
lamp and rubbed it. The genie instantly appeared and Aladdin commanded him to lose no
time in bringing the present that the sultan had
requested. The genie instantly disappeared and
soon returned with forty black slaves, each carrying upon his head a heavy tray, full of pearls,
diamonds, rubies and emeralds. Each basin was
covered with a cloth of silver, on which were
flowers of gold. All these slaves with their
golden basins entirely filled the house as well as
the court in front and a garden behind it.

Aladdin's mother almost fainted when she
saw the great crowd and all the jewels, but
Aladdin asked her to follow the slaves to the
palace and present his gift to the sultan.

No sooner had the first slave turned into the
street than every idle person ran to look, and
by the time the whole procession was on its way,
the crowd was so great that everyone had to
stand in the place where he happened to be.

*Carrying upon his head a heavy tray full of pearls,
diamonds, rubies and emeralds.*

When the first of the eighty slaves arrived
at the gate of the palace, the porters were in
great haste to open it.

When the sultan had been informed of the
arrival of the slaves, he gave orders to have
them admitted. They entered in regular order,
one part going to the right and the other to the
left. After they were all within the hall and

The astonishment of the sultan . . . can hardly be imagined.

had formed a large semicircle before the throne
of the sultan, each of the. black slaves placed
the basin that he carried upon the carpet. Then
they all bowed down until their foreheads
touched the ground. The white slaves also did
the same. Then they all got up and uncovered

the basins which were before them, and then remained standing with their hands crossed upon their breasts.

The astonishment of the sultan at the sight of all these riches can hardly be imagined. After gazing at the shining heaps of jewels, he said to Aladdin's mother, "Go, my good woman, and tell your son that I am waiting with open arms to welcome him!"

Aladdin was so delighted with this news that he could hardly answer his mother. He hastened to his room, shut the door, and having called the genie, he ordered him to take him instantly to a bath. When he had been bathed and perfumed by invisible hands, he was dressed in garments that shone like the sun. The genie also brought him a splendid horse and twenty slaves to march on either side of him on the way to the sultan's palace. All carried purses of gold to scatter among the people.

If there had been a crowd before, there was ten times as great a one now to watch Aladdin as he rode past, and to pick up the gold pieces which were scattered in the street by the slaves. The sultan came down from his throne to greet him, and there was great feasting and joy in the palace. The sultan asked Aladdin if he wished to remain in the palace and be married that day.

The sultan came down from his throne to greet him.

Aladdin replied, "I beg you to permit me to wait until I have built a palace to receive the princess. I request you to point out a suitable place for it near your own."

"My son," answered the sultan, "there is a large open space before my palace and you may take whatever spot you wish, but remember that, to have my happiness complete, I cannot see you united too soon to my daughter."

Aladdin then took leave of the sultan and departed. As soon as he reached his home, he lost no time in again calling the genie. He commanded him to build a beautiful palace on the spot of ground given by the sultan.

Early the next morning the genie appeared. "My lord," said he, "your palace is finished; come and see if it is as you wish." Aladdin found it far more beautiful than even he had hoped for. Words cannot tell the astonishment of the sultan and his household at seeing this wonderful palace.

The marriage of the princess and Aladdin was held the same day with great rejoicing.

For several months there was nothing but happiness, but there was soon to be an end of it.

Aladdin had become very fond of hunting, and there was not a week that he did not go out to follow the chase, and sometimes at a long distance from the city.

About this time his old enemy, the magician, found out by some of his magical arts that Aladdin was enormously rich and much beloved instead of being dead, as he had supposed, in the enchanted cave. He was filled with rage, and immediately set out for China. On arriving there, he went to one of the great merchants and began talking about Aladdin and the wonders of his palace. In this way he learned that Aladdin had gone a-hunting, and was not expected home for several days.

The magician bought a dozen shining new lamps, put them in a basket, and set out for

"Who will change old lamps for new ones?"

Aladdin's palace. When he came near it, he called out, "Who will change old lamps for new ones?"

This brought out a great crowd of people, for they all thought he was foolish to give his bright new lamps for old ones.

When he came under the princess's window, all the slaves laughed as they looked down into the street. "Come," said one of the slaves, "let us see if the old fool means what he says. There is an ugly old lamp on the shelf. Maybe he will give a new one in its place." The princess gave her consent, and away ran one of the slaves with the lamp to the magician who willingly gave in exchange the best he had.

As soon as night arrived, he called the genie of the lamp and commanded him to transport him, the palace, and the princess to the farthest corner of Africa. The order was instantly obeyed.

The grief of the sultan was terrible when he found that the palace and his daughter had disappeared. Soldiers were sent in search of Aladdin.

Aladdin was soon found and taken to the sultan. He would have been beheaded if the sultan had not been afraid of the people, by whom Aladdin was much loved.

"Go, wretch!" cried the sultan. "I grant you your life, but if you ever appear before me again you will be beheaded unless within forty days you bring me tidings of my daughter."

Aladdin left the palace, not knowing which way to turn his steps. At length he stopped at a brook to bathe his eyes. As he stooped down, his foot slipped, and to save himself from falling, he pressed the magician's ring, which he still wore on his finger. The genie of the ring appeared before him saying, "What would you have me do?"

"Oh, mighty genie," cried Aladdin, "take me to the spot where my palace now stands."

Instantly Aladdin found himself beside his own palace, which stood in a meadow not far from a strange city. The princess was then walking in her own chamber, weeping over her misfortune. Happening to look out of the window, she saw Aladdin and made signs to him to be silent. Then she sent a slave to bring him in by a private door. The princess and her husband having kissed each other and shed many tears, Aladdin said, "Tell me, my princess, what has become of an old lamp which I left on this shelf?"

The princess then told how her slave had exchanged it for a new one. She also said that the tyrant in whose power she was always carried that lamp in his bosom. Aladdin was sure that this person was no other than his old enemy, the magician.

After talking a long time, they hit upon a plan for getting back the lamp. Aladdin went into the city and, having changed clothes with a wayfarer, he purchased a powder that would cause instant death if it was swallowed. The princess then invited the magician to sup with her. As she had never been so polite to him before, he was delighted with her kindness. While they were at the table, she ordered a slave to bring two cups of wine which she had prepared. After pretending to taste the one she held in her hand, she asked the magician to change cups, as was the custom between lovers in China. He joyfully seized the goblet and drank the wine which contained the deadly poison, and soon fell senseless.

Aladdin, who was hiding near by, snatched the lamp from the magician's bosom and summoned the genie, who instantly carried the palace back to the place from which it had come.

A few hours after, the sultan, who had risen at break of day, went to the window to look at the place where the palace had been. To his great joy, he saw Aladdin's palace shining in the sun. He called his guards and hastened to embrace his daughter. During a whole week nothing was to be heard but the sound of music and feasting in honor of Aladdin's return with the princess.

Not long after this, the sultan died, and Aladdin and the princess ascended the throne.

The Enchanted
Horse

NEW YEAR'S DAY is a great festival
throughout all Persia. It is celebrated
with great rejoicing, not only in the large cities,
but in every town, village, and hamlet. But the
rejoicing is greatest at the court, where one may
see many wonderful sights. Strangers are invited from the neighboring states, and liberal
rewards are given to those who bring the
best inventions.

On one of these feast days, after the most
skilful inventors of the country had entertained
the king, a Hindu appeared at the foot of the
throne with an artificial horse. It was bridled
and saddled and so well made that, at first sight,
it looked like a living horse.

The Hindu pointed to the horse and said to
the king, "Though I come so late before your

majesty, I can assure you that nothing that has been shown today is as wonderful as this horse, which I beg you to examine."

"I see nothing remarkable in the horse," said the king, "except the natural appearance the workman has given him. The skill of any other workman may do as well or better."

The Hindu replied, "It is not for his outward appearance that I recommend my horse, but for the use I can make of him. If I wish him to carry me through the air to the most distant part of the world he will do so in a very short time. This is the wonder of my horse. Permit me to exhibit his remarkable qualities."

The king, who was fond of everything that was curious, had never seen or heard of anything half as wonderful as this. He told the Hindu that he was ready to see him do what he promised.

The Hindu put his foot into the stirrup and mounted his horse. When he had seated himself in the saddle, he asked the king where he was pleased to send him.

About three miles from the city there was a high mountain that could be seen from the large square in front of the palace. "Do you see that mountain?" said the king, pointing to it. "It is not a great way off, but it is far enough for me to judge of the speed you can make in going and returning. But because it is not possible for the eye to follow you so far, bring me a branch of the palm tree that grows at the top of the mountain as proof that you have been there."

The Hindu turned a peg in the hollow of the horse's neck, and in an instant the horse rose from the ground and carried his rider into the air like lightning. He rose to such a height that even those who had the strongest sight could not follow him.

In less than a quarter of an hour they saw the Hindu coming back with a palm branch in his hand, but before he came entirely down, he took two or three turns in the air, amid the shouts of all the people. Then he landed upon the same spot of ground from which he had set out, without either himself or the horse receiving the least shock. He dismounted, went up to the throne, and laid the branch of the palm tree at the king's feet.

The king felt a great desire to have the horse and persuaded himself that he should not find it difficult to make a bargain with the Hindu. "Judging your horse by his outward appearance," said the king to the Hindu, "I did not think him worth much. To show you how highly I value him now, I will buy him of you."

"I never doubted," replied the Hindu, "that your majesty would set a just value on my work as soon as you had seen it. I also foresaw that you would wish to have the horse, and I am not so fond of him that I could not part with him to please your majesty. But I have a request to make, without which I cannot let him go, and perhaps you will not approve of it."

"I am willing," said the king, "to give you anything you may ask in exchange. You know my kingdom is large and contains many rich and populous cities; I will give you the choice of those you like best, to rule for the rest of your life."

"I am obliged to your majesty for the offer you make me," replied the Hindu, "and cannot thank you enough for your generosity. But I must beg you not to be angry with me for having the boldness to tell you that I cannot resign my horse to you unless I may have your daughter as my wife."

The courtiers laughed at this demand of the Hindu, but the king's oldest son was very angry. The king, however, was of the opinion that he should allow the princess to marry the Hindu.

The prince began to fear that the king would grant the Hindu's demand and said, "I hope your majesty will forgive me for daring to ask

you if it is possible that you should hesitate a
moment in denying the request of such an in-
solent beggar."

"My son," replied the king, "I approve of
your zeal in defending our noble family, but you
do not consider the great value of this horse.
If I should refuse the offer, the Hindu may offer
the horse somewhere else. I regard this horse
as the most wonderful thing in the world, but
before I make a bargain for him, I should be
glad if you would examine the horse and give
me your opinion."

The Hindu heard what the king said and
thought that he was not opposed to taking the
horse at his price. So he expressed much joy,
helped the prince to mount, and showed him how
to guide and manage the horse.

The prince mounted the horse, and as soon as
his feet were in the stirrups, without waiting for
more advice, he turned the peg he had seen the
Hindu use. He mounted into the air as quickly
as an arrow is shot from a bow. In a few moments the king, court, and all the people lost
sight of him. Neither horse nor prince could
anywhere be seen.

The Hindu, alarmed at what had happened,
threw himself on his face before the king and
said, "Your majesty saw that the prince would

not permit me to give him the necessary instructions to manage my horse. He was too anxious to show what he could do, but he does not know how to turn the horse around and bring him back again. Therefore, I ask that I may not be blamed for any accidents that may befall him."

This speech surprised the king, who saw the danger of his son, and he asked the Hindu why he had not called the prince back the moment he went.

"Your majesty saw as well as I with what swiftness the horse and the prince flew away," replied the Hindu. "If I had spoken, he would have been too far away to hear me. If he had heard me, he would not know the way to bring the horse back again because he would not wait to learn. But I hope that the prince will find the other peg; for, as soon as he turns that, the horse will cease to rise, and the prince may then turn him toward any place he pleases."

The king was still frightened at the danger of his son and replied, "I fear that it is doubtful that my son will find the other peg and make the right use of it. May not the horse, instead of lighting on the ground, fall upon some rock, or tumble into the sea with him?"

"Your majesty," replied the Hindu, "the horse crosses seas without ever falling into

them, and always carries his rider wherever he
has a mind to go. And you may be sure that if
the prince finds the other peg, the horse will
carry him to some place of safety."

"If my son does not return safe and sound
in three days' time," said the king, "your head
shall answer for his life."

Then he ordered his officers to keep the Hindu a prisoner. Then he retired to his palace,
grieved because the New Year feast had brought
him so much sorrow.

In the meantime the prince was carried
swiftly through the air, and in less than an
hour's time he was so high up that he could not
clearly see anything on the earth. Then he
began to think of returning and thought to do
it by turning the same peg the other way and
pulling the bridle. But when he found that the
horse still rose with the same swiftness, he was
surprised. He turned the peg several times, first
one way and then the other, but all in vain.
Soon he became aware of the mistake he had
made in not taking time to learn to guide the
horse before he mounted him. He understood
the danger he was in, but it did not take away
his reason. He examined the horse's head and
neck with great care and behind the horse's
right ear found another peg, smaller than the

other. He turned that peg, and was delighted to see that the horse descended in the same manner as he had risen, but not as swiftly.

Night was already darkening the earth when the prince found and turned the small peg, and the horse began to descend. It soon grew quite dark, so that instead of choosing the place where he would land, he was forced to let the bridle lie upon the horse's back and wait patiently till he alighted. He was filled with dread lest he should alight in a desert, a river, or in the sea.

At last, after midnight, the horse alighted. The prince dismounted, faint and hungry, for he had eaten nothing since morning. The first thing he had to do was to find out where he was, and he soon found that he was on the roof of a palace. He groped about and soon found a flight of stairs.

Nobody else would have dared to go down those dark stairs, but nothing could stop him. "I did not come," said he to himself, "to do anybody any harm, and any person who meets me will find that I have no weapons in my hands." After saying this, he went softly down the stairs and, when he came to the landing place, he found a door leading into a great hall with a light in it.

He stopped at the door and, listening, heard no noise except the snoring of some persons who

were fast asleep. He advanced into the room
and saw that the persons who were snoring were
guards, with naked sabres by their sides. This
was enough to show the prince that this was the
guard-chamber of some queen or princess; and
it proved to be the latter.

In the next room was the princess, as was
shown by the light shining through the open
door. The prince advanced on tiptoe, without
waking the guards. The princess lay asleep on a
sofa, and her maids were sleeping on the floor.

The prince fell in love with her at once. He
gently woke her, and the princess opened her
eyes without being frightened. Seeing the
prince, she asked him what was the matter.

The prince bowed his head to the ground,
and said, "Most noble princess, by the most wonderful adventure in the world have I come here.
I am the son of the king of Persia, and yesterday morning I was with my father at his court,
celebrating a solemn feast. Now I am in a
strange country, in danger of my life unless you
have the goodness to give me your protection."

This princess was the princess of Bengal,
eldest daughter of the king of that country, who
had built this palace at a small distance from
his capital so she could enjoy the country. After
she had heard the prince, she replied, "Prince,

you are not in a barbarous country. Hospitality
is as easily found in the kingdom of Bengal as
in the kingdom of Persia."

The princess would not give him a chance to
reply, but spoke to him as follows: "Although I
desire to know by what miracle you have come
here from Persia in so short a time and by what
chance you have been able to come into the palace, I will hear your story later and will now
order my maids to give you some refreshments."

The maids of the princess took wax candles
and conducted the prince to a handsome chamber, where they brought him all sorts of food;
and when he had eaten, they removed the table
and left him to rest.

The princess was so struck with the intelligence and the politeness of the prince that she
could not sleep. When her maids came back to
her room, she asked them if they had taken care
of the prince and what they thought of him.

The maids answered: "We do not know what
you may think of him, but we think you would be
very happy if the king should marry you to so
amiable a prince, for there is none in all Bengal
to be compared with him."

This flattering discourse was not displeasing
to the princess, but she only told them not to
talk such nonsense.

Next day the princess dressed herself very carefully and sent to know if the prince was awake so she could pay him a visit.

The prince had rested from the fatigue of his journey, and when the lady in waiting had told her errand, he replied, "It shall be as the princess thinks fit. I am here to do exactly as she wishes."

As soon as the princess understood that the prince waited for her, she went to pay him a visit. After wishing him good day, the princess said, "Through my impatience to hear the surprising adventure which brought you here, I have come to this room so that we may not be interrupted. Therefore I beg you to begin at once."

The prince began with the feast, relating all the things that might interest her. After a while he came to the enchanted horse. The description of it convinced the princess that nothing else in all the world could be so remarkable.

For two whole months the prince remained the guest of the princess, taking part in all the amusements she arranged for him. But after that time he begged permission to return to his father.

"And, princess," said the prince, "in order that you may not doubt the truth of what I say,

The prince turned the horse toward Persia.

I hope you will not be offended when I ask you
to come with me to visit my father."

The princess at once consented to this. The
only difficulty was that she thought the prince
did not know very well how to manage the horse,
and she was afraid of having some accident.
But the prince removed her fear by telling her
that she could trust herself with him. After the
experience he had had, he defied the Hindu
himself to manage the horse any better.

The next morning before daybreak, they
went out on the roof of the palace. The prince
turned the horse towards Persia and placed him
where the princess could easily climb up to the
saddle behind him. When she was safely seated
with her arms around the prince's waist, he
turned the peg, and the horse mounted into the
air with his usual speed and in two hours' time
they came in sight of the capital of Persia.

The prince would not alight in the great
square whence he had set out, nor in the sultan's
palace, but directed his course towards a palace
at a little distance from the town. He led the
princess into a handsome apartment where he
asked her to wait while he went and informed
his father of their arrival. He ordered the
housekeeper of the palace to provide the princess with anything she wished.

As he passed through the streets, he was welcomed by the shouts of the people, who were overjoyed to see him again. His father was at court when the prince appeared before him in the midst of his council. The sultan, embracing him with tears of joy, asked what had become of the Hindu's horse.

This question gave the prince an opportunity to tell of the danger he had been in when the horse mounted into the air with him, but how he had arrived at last at the palace of the princess of Bengal. He told of the kind reception he had met with there and how, after promising to marry the princess, he had persuaded her to come with him to Persia. "But, sir," added the prince, "I have promised that you would not refuse your consent, and have brought her with me on the Hindu's horse to a palace where your majesty often goes. I have left her there till I could return and assure her that my promise was not in vain."

After these words the prince fell on his face before the king to gain his consent, but his father raised him up, embraced him a second time, and said, "My son, I not only consent to your marriage with the princess, but I will go and meet her myself and celebrate your wedding this day."

Then the king gave orders for his court to make preparations for the wedding and gave orders for the Hindu to be let out of prison. When the Hindu was brought before the king, he said, "I secured your person so that your life might answer for that of my son, but, thank Heaven! I have found him again. Now take your horse and go, and never let me see your face again."

The Hindu had learned of those who brought him out of prison that the prince had returned and had brought a princess with him on his horse, and was also informed of the place where he had left her.

As soon as he was out of the king's presence, he went direct to the palace and told the housekeeper that he came from the king and the prince to bring the princess of Bengal to the city.

The housekeeper knew the Hindu, and knew that the king had imprisoned him. She believed what he said because he was at liberty. She took him to the princess and, as soon as the princess understood that he came from the prince, she consented to go with him.

The Hindu, overjoyed at his success, mounted his horse, took the princess before him, turned the peg, and presently the horse rose into the air with him and the princess.

Presently the horse rose into the air with him and the princess.

At the same time the king, followed by his court, was on the way to the palace where the princess had been left. The prince had ridden on before to prepare the princess to receive him when the Hindu, to revenge himself for the ill-treatment he had received, passed over their heads with his prize.

When the king saw this he stopped. His grief was more keen because it was not in his power to punish the offender.

The Hindu was little moved by their curses and continued on his way, while the king returned to his palace.

But what was the prince's grief to see the Hindu carry away the princess whom he loved so dearly! He was thunderstruck at the sight. He could not decide what to do, and so continued his way to the palace where he had left his princess.

Soon he dressed himself in the suit of a dervish priest, took the box of jewels which he had brought as a present to the princess, and left the palace. He was uncertain which way to go, but resolved not to return till he had found the princess and brought her back again.

In the meantime the Hindu managed his horse so well that he arrived early in the evening at a wood near the capital of the kingdom of

Cashmere. Being hungry and thinking that the princess was hungry also, he alighted in an open part of the wood and left the princess on a grassy spot by a little stream of clear, fresh water.

During the Hindu's absence, the princess, who knew that she was in the power of a wicked man, thought of running away from him; but she was so weak from want of food that she was forced to stay where she was.

When the Hindu returned, she did not wait to be asked twice, but ate with him and soon recovered her strength. She saw a company of horsemen approaching and called to them for help. They happened to be the king of Cashmere and his attendants, returning from hunting.

The princess, who did not know the rank of the person who had come to her relief, said to the king, "Sir, whoever you are that Heaven has sent to my assistance, have pity on a poor princess, and take me away from this wicked Hindu. He has carried me away from Persia and has brought me here on his enchanted horse."

The princess had no need to say any more to convince the king of Cashmere that she told the truth. Being enraged at the insolence of the Hindu, the king of Cashmere ordered his guards to surround him and cut off his head. This was done immediately.

The princess, thus delivered from the Hindu, fell into another danger. The king ordered a horse for her and carried her with him to his palace, where he lodged her in a finely furnished room next his own and gave her a number of women slaves to attend her.

Before he left her, he said, "As I am certain that you must want rest, I take my leave of you till tomorrow, when you will be better able to tell me about this strange adventure."

The princess was full of joy at her deliverance. She was sure that the king of Cashmere would send her back to Persia when she told him her story and asked that favor of him. She was very much mistaken, for the king of Cashmere had resolved to marry her the next day. He had ordered rejoicings to be made at daybreak by beating of drums and sounding of trumpets, which echoed throughout the city.

The princess was awakened by the noise. When the king came to inquire after her health, he told her that all those rejoicings were in honor of their wedding. This frightened the princess so much that she fainted away.

The women slaves ran to her assistance, and the king did all he could to bring her to herself again. When her senses returned, she decided to pretend she was seized with madness rather than break the promise she had made to the prince by consenting to marry the king of Cashmere.

When the king found that her condition became worse, he left her with her women, after charging them to take great care of her. He often sent to ask how she was, but received answer that she was worse instead of better. When night came, she seemed much worse than she had all day.

The princess talked wildly and acted strangely next day and the following ones, so that the king was obliged to send for all the physicians of his court to ask them if they could cure her.

The princess feared that if she let the physicians feel her pulse, they would soon know that she was in a good state of health, and that her madness was only pretended. So she flew into such a rage that she seemed ready to tear out their eyes if they came near her, and none of them dared approach her.

When the king of Cashmere saw that his court physicians could not cure her, he called in the most skilful doctors in the city, but they had no better success. Afterwards he sent for the most famous physicians in the kingdom, but they met with no better reception than the others. Afterwards the king sent messengers

The most famous physicians met with no success.

to the neighboring courts, promising a handsome reward to any one who should cure the princess.

Many physicians came and undertook the cure; but none of them succeeded, since it was a case that did not depend on their skill but on the will of the princess herself.

Meantime the prince, disguised as a dervish, had traveled through many countries and endured much fatigue, not knowing which way to go. He made inquiry after the princess at every place he came to, till at last he heard the people talk of a princess of Bengal, who went mad on the day of her marriage with the king of Cashmere. As soon as he heard this he set out for the kingdom of Cashmere, and on his arrival at the capital he went and lodged at an inn, where he was again told the story of the princess and the unhappy fate of the Hindu. The prince knew that she was the princess he had so long sought.

The prince being informed of all these things, provided himself with a physician's robe so that he passed for a physician, and went to the king's palace. Presenting himself to the chief officer, he told him that perhaps he might be looked upon as very bold to offer to attempt the cure of the princess after so many had failed, but he hoped to find the right remedy.

It was a long time since any physician had offered himself, and the king of Cashmere had begun to lose hope of ever seeing the princess restored to her former health. He ordered the officer to bring in the physician at once.

The prince was presented to the king of Cashmere in the robe and disguise of a physician, and the king, without wasting any time, told him that the princess could not bear the sight of a physician without falling into the most violent anger. So he took him into a private room, from which, through a window, he could see the princess without being seen.

There the prince saw the lovely princess with tears in her eyes, and he knew that her illness was only pretended. When he came away he told the king that she was not incurable. But first he must speak to her in private, and he hoped she would hear him.

The king ordered the princess' door to be opened, and the prince went in. As soon as the princess saw him she took him for a physician and rose up in a rage. He only moved towards her and said in a low voice, "Princess, I am the prince of Persia, and have come to set you free."

The princess knew the sound of his voice at once, and a look of pleasure overspread her face. Fortunately her surprise deprived her for the time of speech and gave the prince time to tell her of his grief when he saw the Hindu carry her away. He told her he had vowed never to return home till he had found her, and by what good fortune he had at last found her in the palace of the king of Cashmere.

At last the princess was able to tell how she had been rescued from the Hindu by the king as he was returning from hunting. She told him how she had been treated by the king because of his haste to marry her that very day, without even asking her consent. She also told how she had fainted and pretended madness to save herself from the king.

Then the prince asked her if she knew what had become of the horse after the Hindu's death. She answered that she knew not what orders the sultan had given about it, but believed he would take care of it.

As the prince did not doubt that the king had the horse, he told the princess he intended making use of it to carry them both back to Persia. After they had talked over plans for their escape, they agreed that the princess should next day receive the king civilly, but without speaking to him.

The king was overjoyed when the prince told him the effect of his first visit on the princess.

And next day, when the princess received him in such a pleasant manner, he looked upon the prince as the greatest physician in the world and was sure she would recover her health.

The prince, who went with the king, asked him if he might inquire how the princess came into the kingdom of Cashmere alone, since her country was so far off?

The king, who did not suspect the prince's reason for asking this question, concealed nothing, but told him much the same story as the princess had told; and added that the enchanted horse was kept safe in his treasury as a great curiosity, although he did not know the use of it.

"The information which your majesty gives me," replied the pretended physician, "provides me a means of curing the princess. As she was brought here on this horse, and the horse is enchanted, she has received some of the enchantment, which must be driven back into the horse. If your majesty should wish to see the most surpassing sight that ever was seen, let the horse be brought into the great square before the palace and leave the rest to me. In a few moments' time I promise to show you the princess of Bengal as well in body and mind as she ever was in her life."

Early the next day the enchanted horse was placed in the great square before the palace. A report was spread through the town that there was something wonderful to be seen, and crowds of people assembled.

The king of Cashmere, surrounded by all his ministers, sat on a platform erected on purpose. The princess of Bengal, attended by a number of ladies, went up to the enchanted horse and the women helped her to mount. When she was seated in the saddle and had the bridle in her hand, the pretended physician placed around the horse a great many pans full of fire. Then he cast a pleasant perfume into the pans, and with his hands upon his breast ran three times around the horse, pronouncing certain words. In a moment the pans sent forth a dark cloud of smoke, which so surrounded the princess that neither she nor the horse could be seen.

Without a moment's delay the prince nimbly jumped up behind her and turned the peg. Just as the horse rose into the air with them, he shouted, "King of Cashmere, when you wish to marry a princess, first obtain her consent."

Thus the prince with the princess arrived that same day in the capital of Persia and alighted on the grounds of the palace. The king delayed the marriage no longer than was necessary, and after the days of rejoicing were over, his first care was to appoint an ambassador to go and give the king of Bengal an account of what had happened and to ask his approval of the marriage. The king of Bengal took this as an honor and granted the request with pleasure.

Adventure of the Caliph Haroun al-Raschid

ONCE as the Caliph Haroun al-Raschid, with Grand Vizier Giafer, disguised as a merchant, was proceeding across the bridge that spans the river Euphrates in the middle of the city of Bagdad, he met an old man who was blind, begging for alms. The caliph gave him a piece of gold, and was much surprised at the old man's request. For he said: "Pray, sir, give me a box on the ears, otherwise I shall be unable to accept your alms without breaking a solemn vow."

After some hesitation, the caliph obeyed this strange request, gave him a very slight blow, and continued on his walk. When they had gone a little way the caliph said to the vizier, "Return and tell that blind man to come to my palace tomorrow at the hour of afternoon prayer, for I would fain hear his history, which must be strange."

The vizier hastened to obey and then resumed his walk with the caliph.

When they came into the town, they found in a square a great crowd of spectators looking at a handsome young man who was mounted on a mare which he drove and urged full speed around the palace, spurring and whipping the poor creature in a cruel manner. The caliph was much distressed. He bade the vizier summon the young man to the palace also that he might know why he ill-treated the mare so.

They then turned towards the palace, and on the way thither the caliph espied a handsome building which he had noticed before. "Who lives there?" said he. The vizier made inquiries and learned that it was one Cogia Hassan, surnamed Alhabbal, which means ropemaker, since that was his trade. The caliph was much interested and commanded the vizier to summon him also to the palace on the morrow.

The next day, therefore, the three men repaired to the palace, where they were introduced into the caliph's presence by the grand vizier.

They all three prostrated themselves before the throne, and when they rose up, the caliph asked the blind man his name. He answered, "It is Baba Abdalla."

"Baba Abdalla," said the caliph, "tell me why you require those who give you alms to give you a box on the ear. The blind man, having bowed low, replied: "Sir, I will tell you. Then you will see the apparently strange action is but a slight penance for a great crime of which I am guilty." Whereupon he told the story of the Forty Camels.

The Story of the
Forty Camels

I WAS born at Bagdad and, at an early age finding myself in possession of considerable wealth, soon began to trade with all the cities of your realm.

One of my journeys led me to Bussorah. When I was returning with my laden camels, I met a dervish with whom, after we had each satisfied the other's curiosity, I sat down to eat.

During our repast the dervish told me that he knew of a spot close by where there were such immense riches that if all my four score camels were loaded with the gold and jewels that might be taken from it, they would not be missed.

I was delighted by what I heard, and begged the dervish to conduct me to the spot. Whereupon he replied: "I am ready to conduct you to the place where the treasure lies, and we will

load your four score camels with jewels and gold
as much as they can carry, on condition that
when they are so loaded, you will let me have one
half and you be contented with the other. After
that we will separate and take our camels where
we may think fit. You see there is nothing but
what is strictly equitable in this division; for if
you give me forty camels, you will procure by
my means wherewithal to purchase thousands."

Although avarice made me loath to forego
so much, I had no alternative but to accept the
terms the dervish offered. When he had heard
my decision he led me to the place.

It was a valley situated between two high
mountains, so secluded that there was no fear
of discovery. When we arrived, the dervish
bade me stop my camels. He quickly collected
some sticks and proceeded to kindle a fire, pronouncing over it an incantation. A dense smoke
arose from the fire, and when this had cleared
away I perceived that the sides of the cliff opposite to us had rolled back revealing a magnificent palace in the side of the mountain, with
great heaps of treasure lying about.

I was as rapacious as a bird of prey in the
way I seized the gold and filled my sacks, until
I perceived that the dervish paid more heed to
the jewels. Then I followed his example, so that

A magnificent palace in the side of the mountain.

we took away more jewels than gold. Among
other things the dervish took a small golden
vase, which he showed me contained nothing
more than glutinous ointment. After we had
loaded our camels he closed the rock by using
some mystic words.

We now divided our camels, each taking forty, and traveled together till we came to the great road where we were to part, the dervish to go to Bussorah, and I to Bagdad. We embraced each other with great joy and, taking our leave, pursued our different routes.

I had not gone far before the demon of ingratitude and envy took possession of my heart, and I deplored the loss of my camels, but much more the riches wherewith they were loaded. The dervish, said I to myself, has no occasion for all this wealth, since he is master of the treasure and may have as much as he pleases; so I gave myself up to the blackest ingratitude and determined immediately to take the camels with their loading from him.

To execute this design I called to him as loud as I could, giving him to understand that I had something material to say to him, and made a sign to him to stop, which he accordingly did after a few moments.

When I came up to him, I said, "Brother, I had no sooner parted from you, but a thought came into my head, which neither of us had reflected on before. You are a recluse dervish, used to live in tranquillity, disengaged from all the cares of the world, and intent only upon serving God. You know not, perhaps, what trouble

I called to him as loud as I could.

you have taken upon yourself to take care of so
many camels. If you would take my advice, you
would keep but thirty; you will find them suf-
ficiently troublesome to manage. Take my
word; I have had experience."

The dervish, who seemed rather afraid of me, at once made me choose ten from his forty. This I promptly did and drove them after my forty. I was much surprised by his ready compliance, and my avarice increased. "Brother," said I, "thirty camels are too many for you to manage since you are not used to the work, therefore I beg of you relieve yourself of ten more."

My discourse had the desired effect upon the dervish, who gave me, without any hesitation, the other ten camels; so that he had but twenty left, and I was master of sixty and might boast of greater riches than any sovereign princes. Anyone would have thought I should now have been content; but I became more greedy and desirous of the other twenty camels.

I redoubled my solicitations and importunities to make the dervish condescend to grant me ten of the twenty, which he did with a good grace. As to the other ten he had left, I embraced him, kissed his feet, and caressed him, conjuring him not to refuse me, but to complete the obligation I should ever be under to him, so that at length he crowned my joy by giving me them also. Then a thought came into my head that the little box of unguent which the dervish showed me had something in it more precious than all the riches I had. So I longed to possess it, and said: "What will you do with that little box of ointment? It seems such a trifle, it is not worth carrying away. I request you to make me a present of it; for what occasion has a dervish, as you are, who has renounced the vanities of the world, for perfumes or scented unguents?"

Would to heaven he had refused me that box; but if he had, I was stronger than he, and resolved to have taken it from him by force, that it might not be said he had carried away the smallest part of the treasure.

The dervish readily pulled it out of his bosom and, presenting it to me with the best grace in the world, said: "Here, take it, brother, and be content. If I could do more for you, you needed but to have asked me."

When I had the box in my hand, I opened it, and looking at the unguent, said to him: "Since you are so good, I am sure you will not refuse the favor to tell me the particular use of this ointment."

"The use is very surprising and wonderful," replied the dervish. "If you apply a little of it round the left eye, you will see at once all the treasures contained in the bosom of the earth; but if you apply it to the right eye, it will make you blind."

At my request the dervish applied some of the ointment to my left eye, when I found that he had indeed spoken truly. I saw incalculable riches and longed to grasp them all. But, thinking that the dervish merely wished to hide something from me when he said that, if applied to the right eye, loss of sight would ensue, I bade him put some round that eye.

"Pray remember," said the dervish, "that you will immediately become blind."

Far from being persuaded of the truth of what the dervish said, I imagined, on the contrary, that there was some new mystery which he meant to hide from me. "Brother," replied I, smiling, "I see plainly you wish to mislead me; it is not natural that this ointment should have two such contrary effects."

"The matter is as I tell you," replied the dervish.

I would not believe the dervish, who spoke like an honest man. My insurmountable desire of seeing at my will all the treasures in the world, and perhaps of enjoying those treasures to the extent I coveted, had such an effect on me that I would not hearken to his remonstrances.

"Grant me this last favor," I pleaded. "Whatever happens I will not lay the blame on you but take it upon myself alone."

The dervish made all the resistance possible but, seeing that I was able to force him to do it, he took a little of the fatal ointment and applied it to my right eye. But alas! when I came to open it, I could distinguish nothing with either eye, and became blind as you now see me.

"Ah! dervish," I exclaimed in agony, "what you forewarned me of has proved but too true. Fatal curiosity," added I, "insatiable desire of riches, into what an abyss of miseries have they cast me! But you, dear brother, who are so charitable and good, among the many wonderful secrets you are acquainted with, have you not one to restore to me my sight again?"

"Miserable wretch!" answered the dervish. "If you would have been advised by me you would have avoided this misfortune, but you have your deserts. The blindness of your mind was the cause of the loss of your eyes. Pray to God, therefore, if you believe there is one; it is He alone that can restore it to you. He gave you riches, of which you were unworthy, and on that account takes them from you again and will, by my hands, give them to men not so ungrateful as yourself."

The dervish left me to myself overwhelmed with confusion and plunged in inexpressible grief. After he had collected my camels, he

drove them away and pursued the road to Bussorah.

I cried out loudly as he was departing and
entreated him not to leave me in that miserable
condition, but he was deaf to my prayers and
entreaties. Thus deprived of sight and all I had
in the world, I should have died with affliction
and hunger if the next day a caravan returning
from Bussorah had not received me charitably
and brought me back to Bagdad. After this
manner was I reduced to beggary without re-
source. But to expiate my offence against God,
I enjoined myself, by way of penance, a box on
the ear from every charitable person who should
commiserate my condition.

Thus Baba Abdalla ended his story.

"Baba Abdalla," said the caliph, "you may
cease to beg publicly, for in future my grand
vizier will pay you four silver dirhens, accompanied with your self-imposed penance, to show
my appreciation of your remorse."

At these words, Baba Abdalla prostrated
himself before the caliph's throne, returned him
thanks, and wished him all happiness and prosperity.

The Story of
Syed Nouman

THE caliph then commanded the young man to tell why he so ill-treated the mare, whereupon he spoke as follows:

Sir, my name is Syed Nouman, and my history is a strange one. I married a beautiful woman, named Amine, whose strange conduct has caused my grief.

As it is the custom for us to marry without seeing or knowing whom we are to espouse, your majesty is sensible that a husband has no reason to complain when he finds that the wife who has been chosen for him is not horribly ugly and deformed, and that her carriage, wit, and behavior make amends for any slight bodily imperfections.

The first time I saw my wife with her face uncovered, we regarded each other with mutual

admiration. My wife never ate anything except
a little rice, which she consumed grain by grain,
carrying the food to her mouth with a silver
bodkin. As I knew that this was not sufficient
to support life, I became suspicious and determined to watch her. Therefore I lay awake at
night, hoping to discover an explanation of the
mystery, and at last I was rewarded.

One night, when she thought me fast asleep,
she got out of bed softly, dressed herself with
great precaution, and went softly out of the
room. When she was gone, I arose, threw my
cloak over my shoulders, and followed her till
I saw her enter a burying ground just by our
house. There she joined a ghoul, of whose hor-
rid feast I saw her partake. Much distressed at
this sight, I returned home to bed, scarcely able
to abide my wife's presence when she returned
as noiselessly as she had gone.

The next day I went out early and remained
away all day, but when I returned, Amine ordered dinner to be served and ate the rice in the
same odd manner she did on previous occasions.
Unable to look upon her in silence, I said: "Are
not my feasts as good as those provided by
ghouls?"

At these words Amine's face became terrible
and she cried in fury: "Wretch, receive the pun-

ishment of thy prying curiosity, and become a dog!"

Amine had no sooner pronounced these words, than I was immediately transformed into a dog. My wife then took up a stick and beat me unmercifully. After this she opened the door, and I rushed howling down the street pursued by a great many dogs which snapped at me ferociously. To escape from them I ran into a shop where sheep's heads were exposed to view. Later, seeing a lot of dogs waiting outside, I joined them and got something to eat. On the next day I went to a baker's shop, where the master received me kindly and allowed me to stay with him.

I had lived some time with this baker, when a woman came one day into the shop to buy some bread. She gave my master a piece of bad money among some good, which he returned and requested her to exchange. The woman refused to take it again, and affirmed it to be good. The baker maintained the contrary and, in the dispute, told the woman he was sure that the piece of money was so visibly bad that his dog could distinguish it. Having called me, he said: "See, and tell me which of these pieces is bad."

I looked over all the pieces of money, then set my paw upon that which was bad and sep-

arated it from the rest, looking in my master's
face to show it to him.

The baker was not a little surprised, and
soon my fame became so great that the shop
was crowded with customers. One day a woman
entered and, having tested my ability, she beck-
oned me to follow her home. I understood what
she meant and went readily enough. We soon
reached her house, when she bade me enter and
conducted me to her daughter, who was an enchantress.

"Daughter," said she, "this is the famous
dog, which I think is a man in disguise. Say, am
I right?"

"You are," replied the young lady, "and I will
quickly remove the enchantment."

The young lady arose from her sofa, put her
hand into a basin of water, and throwing some
upon me, said, "If thou wert born a dog, remain
so; but if thou wert born a man, resume thy
former shape, by the virtue of this water."

At that instant the enchantment was broken,
and I became restored to my natural form.

I thanked my deliverer and was about to
depart, when she said: "Take of this water, and
when you go home, throw it over your cruel wife
and say, 'Receive the reward of your evil
deeds.'"

I did as she commanded, and immediately Amine became changed into a mare—the same you saw me upon yesterday. This is the punishment I inflict upon her. You have now heard my history as you desired.

So ended the story of Syed Nouman. Whereupon the caliph spake:

"Your wife indeed deserves her punishment, yet I would fain see you reconciled were I sure that she would abstain from her evil ways, since I think she has suffered enough."

Having spoken thus, he turned to Cogia Hassan, who told his story in obedience to the caliph's command.

The Story of
Cogia Hassan

SIR, it is to my two friends Saadi and Saad that I, Cogia Hassan Alhabbal, the ropemaker, owe all my present wealth. I will now tell you in what manner I acquired the riches. Saadi and Saad could never agree as to the chief factor of happiness. Saadi, who is very rich, was always of opinion that no man could be happy in this world without wealth, to live independent of everyone. Saad was of a different opinion. He agreed that riches were necessary to comfort, but maintained that the happiness of a man's life consisted in virtue, without any further eagerness after worldly goods than what was requisite for decent subsistence and benevolent purposes.

One day, as they were talking upon this subject, as I have since been informed by them both,

Saadi said: "I will make an experiment to convince you, by giving, for example, a sum of money to some artisan." And as they happened to be passing my shop, they saw me at work.

Then Saad said: "There is a man," pointing to me, "whom I can remember a long time working at his trade of ropemaking, and in the same poverty: he is a worthy subject for your liberality and a proper person to make your experiment upon."

The two friends came to me and told me the object of their visit, after which Saadi pulled a purse out of his bosom, and, putting it into my hands, said: "Here, take this purse; you will find it contains two hundred pieces of gold. I pray God bless you with them and give you grace to make the good use of them I desire. Believe me, my friend Saad and I shall both take great pleasure in finding they may contribute towards making you more happy than you now are."

After I had duly thanked them, the two friends departed, and I returned to my work to think over my good fortune. Then I began to wonder what I should do with the money to keep it safe, for I had in my poor house neither box nor cupboard to lock it up in, nor any other place where I could be sure it would not be discovered if I concealed it.

In this perplexity I sewed up the gold, except ten pieces which I kept out to provide for my immediate wants, in the folds of the linen which went about my turban. I then bought a fresh stock of hemp and afterwards, as my family had eaten no meat for a long time, I went and bought something for supper.

As I was carrying home the meat I had bought, a famished vulture flew upon me, and would have taken it away if I had not held it very fast. So fierce was the struggle that my turban fell on the ground.

The vulture immediately let go his hold and, seizing my turban, flew away with it. I cried out so loud that I alarmed all the men, women, and children in the neighborhood, who joined their shouts and cries to make the vulture quit his hold. But our cries did not avail; he carried off my turban, and we soon lost sight of him. It would have been in vain for me to fatigue myself with running after him.

I went home very melancholy at the loss of my money. I was obliged to buy a new turban, which diminished the small remainder of the ten pieces, for I had laid out several in hemp. The little that was left was not sufficient to give me reason to indulge the great hopes I had conceived.

While the remainder of the ten pieces lasted, my little family and I lived better than usual; but I soon relapsed into the same poverty. However, I never murmured nor repined; though, when I told my neighbors I had lost a hundred and ninety pieces of gold, they only laughed at me.

When, at the end of six months, the two friends returned to my shop, I felt very much ashamed of the incredible story I had to tell them. Saadi scoffed at my word and said: "Hassan, you joke, and would deceive me. What have vultures to do with turbans? They only search for something to satisfy their hunger."

"Sir," I replied, "I can call witnesses to prove my words."

Then, to my surprise, Saad took my part and told Saadi a great many stories of vultures, some of which he affirmed he knew to be true, insomuch that at last Saadi pulled out his purse and counted out two hundred pieces of gold into my hand. I put them into my bosom for want of a purse, vowing to take more care of this generous present, for which he would not receive one word of thanks, but walked on quietly with his friend.

As soon as they were gone, I left off work and went home. Finding neither my wife nor

Saadi pulled out his purse and counted out two hundred pieces of gold into my hand.

children within, I pulled out my money, put ten pieces by, and laid the rest in a vessel of bran which stood in the corner. My wife came home soon after, and as I had but little hemp in the house, I told her I would go out to buy some, without saying anything to her about the two friends.

While I was absent, a sandman, who sells scouring-earth, passed through our street. My wife wanted some but, as she had no money, she asked him if he would make an exchange of some earth for some bran. This he agreed to do and took the pot and bran along with him.

When I returned, I noticed that the vessel was gone, and I asked my wife what had become of it. She told me the bargain she had made with the sandman, which she thought to be a very good one.

I then told her what a serious mistake she had made and reproached her bitterly.

My wife was like one distracted when she knew what a fault she had committed. She cried, beat her breast, and tore her hair and clothes.

"Unhappy wretch that I am," cried she, "am I fit to live after so dreadful a mistake? Where shall I find this sandman? I know him not. I never saw him in our street before. Oh! husband," added she, "you were much to blame to be so reserved in a matter of such importance!"

"Wife," said I, "moderate your grief; by your howling you will alarm the neighborhood, and they will only laugh at, instead of pitying us."

After this I did not look forward with pleasure to the return of the two friends. In fact, when I saw them coming towards me, I could not look them in the face, but told what had happened with downcast eyes and a sorry heart. They listened in silence, and after I had finished the narration of my misfortunes I added: "I see, sir, that it has pleased God, whose ways are secret and impenetrable, that I should not be enriched by your liberality but that I must remain poor. However, the obligation is the same as if it had wrought the desired effect."

After these words I was silent; and Saadi, turning about to his friend Saad, said: "You may now make your experiment and let me see that there are ways, besides giving money, to make a poor man's fortune. Let Hassan be the man. I dare say, whatever you may give him, he will not be richer than he was with four hundred pieces of gold."

Saad had a piece of lead in his hand, which he showed Saadi. "You saw me," said he, "take up this piece of lead, which I found on the ground. I will give it to Hassan, and you shall see what it is worth."

Saadi burst out laughing at Saad. "What is that bit of lead worth?" said he—"a farthing? What can Hassan do with that?"

Saad presented it to me, and said, "Take it, Hassan; let Saadi laugh. You will tell us some news of the good luck it has brought you one time or another." I thought Saad was in jest, and had a mind to divert himself. However, I took the lead and thanked him. The two friends pursued their walk, and I fell to work again.

At night when I pulled off my clothes to go to bed, the piece of lead, which I had never thought of from the time he gave it me, tumbled out of my pocket. I took it up and laid it on the place that was nearest me. The same night it happened that a fisherman, a neighbor, mending his nets, found a piece of lead wanting. It being too late to buy any, as the shops were shut, he called to his wife and bade her inquire among the neighbors for a piece. She went from door to door on both sides of the street, but could not get any, and returned to tell her husband her ill success. He asked her if she had been to several of their neighbors, naming them, and among the rest my house. "No, indeed," said the wife, "I have not been there. That was too far off; and if I had gone, do you think I should have found any? I know by experience they never have anything when one wants it."

"No matter," said the fisherman, "you must go there; for though you have been there a hundred times before without getting anything, you may chance to obtain what we want now."

The fisherman's wife went out grumbling, came and knocked at my door, and waked me out of a sound sleep. "Hassan," said she, "my huband wants a bit of lead to load his nets with, and if you have a piece, desires you to give it to him."

Remembering the piece which Saad had given me, I told my neighbor I had some, and if she would stay a moment my wife should give it to her. Accordingly, my wife, who was awakened by the noise as well as myself, got up, and groping about where I directed her, found the lead, opened the door, and gave it to the fisherman's wife, who was so overjoyed that she promised my wife that in return for the kindness she did her and her husband we should have the first cast of the nets.

The fisherman was so much rejoiced to see the lead, which he so little expected, that he much approved his wife's promise. He finished mending his nets and went fishing two hours before day, according to custom. At the first throw he caught but one fish, about a yard long and proportionable in thickness, but afterwards had a great many successful casts; though of all the fish he took, none equaled the first in size.

The next morning, mindful of his wife's promise, he came to me, holding in his hand a fine fish, and said: "Neighbor, my wife promised you last night, in return for your kindness, whatever fish I should catch at my first throw. It pleased God to send me no more than this one for you, which, such as it is, I desire you to accept. I wish it had been better."

"Neighbor," said I, "the bit of lead which I sent you was such a trifle that it ought not to be valued at so high a rate. Neighbors should assist each other in their little wants. I have done no more for you than I should have expected from you had I been in your situation. Therefore I would refuse your present if I were not persuaded you gave it me freely, and that I should offend you. Since you will have it so, I take it and return you my hearty thanks."

After these civilities, I took the fish and carried it home to my wife, who said that she could not cook it whole, as we had no utensil large enough. "Do it as you can," said I, "for any

He came to me, holding in his hand a fine fish.

way it will be good." While my wife was preparing it, she found a large crystal, which she took for a piece of glass, and gave it to the youngest of our children for a plaything, and his brothers and sisters handed it about from one to another to admire its brightness and beauty.

At night, when the lamp was lighted and the children were still playing with the crystal, they perceived that it gave a light when my wife, who was getting them their supper, stood between them and the lamp. They began to squabble over its possession, so I called to the eldest to know what was the matter. He told me it was about a piece of glass which shone in the dark. Curious to test the truth of this, I put out the lamp, and found out that they were quite right.

"Look," said I, "this is another advantage which Saad's piece of lead has procured. We shall now be saved the expense of oil."

When the children saw the lamp was put out and the bit of glass supplied the place, they cried out so loud and made so great a noise from astonishment that it aroused our neighbors, whose room was only separated by a thin partition. This neighbor was a Jew, a jeweler and very wealthy, and the next day he sent his wife to complain of being disturbed out of their first sleep. "Good neighbor, Rachel," which was the Jewess's name, said my wife, "I am very sorry for what happened, and hope you will excuse it. You know it was caused by the children, and they will laugh and cry for a trifle. Come in, and I will show you what was the occasion of the noise."

The Jewess went in with her, and my wife, taking the diamond (for such it really was, and a very extraordinary one) out of the chimney, put it into her hands. "See here," said she, "it was this piece of glass that caused all the noise;" and while the Jewess, who understood all sorts of precious stones, was examining the diamond with admiration, my wife told her how she found it.

"Indeed, Ayesha," which was my wife's name, said the jeweler's wife, giving her the diamond again, "I believe, as you do, it is a piece of glass, but as it is more beautiful than common glass. I have just such another piece at home. I will buy it, if you will sell it."

The children, who heard them talking of selling their plaything, presently interrupted their conversation, crying and begging their mother not to part with it. To quiet them, she promised she would not.

The Jewess being thus prevented in her intended swindling bargain by my children, went away, but first whispered to my wife, who followed her to the door, if she had a mind to sell it, not to show it to anybody without acquainting her.

No sooner had the Jewess informed her husband of the find she had made than he sent her to offer my wife twenty pieces of gold for the glass. But my wife would not part with it until she had consulted me. As I happened to come home at that instant, my wife told me of the offer. I paused for a while, reflecting upon Saad's assurances that the piece of lead would make my fortune, but the Jewess, fancying that the low price she had offered was the reason I made no reply, said, "I will give you fifty, neighbor, if that will do."

As soon as I found that she rose so suddenly from twenty to fifty, I told her that I expected a great deal more. "Well, neighbor," said she, "I will give you a hundred, but that is so much I know not whether my husband will approve my offering it." At this new advance, I told her I would have a hundred thousand pieces of gold for it. I saw plainly that the diamond, for such I now guessed it must be, was worth a great deal more, but to oblige her and her husband, as they were neighbors, I would limit myself to that price. If they refused to give it, other jewelers should have it, who would give a great deal more.

The Jewess confirmed me in this resolution by her eagerness to conclude a bargain; and by coming up at several biddings to fifty thousand pieces, which I refused. "I can offer you no more," said she, "without my husband's consent. He will be at home at night, and I would beg the favor of you to let him see it." I promised.

When the Jew himself came in the evening, I remained firm to my offer. Although he haggled, I refused to accept less than I had said. In the end, he decided to pay what I asked and deposited two bags, each containing one thousand pieces of gold, as surety, promising to pay the rest on the morrow. This he did according to our agreement, and I handed him the diamond.

In spite of my wife's request for rich clothing, I vowed not to lavish my wealth, but to lay the foundations of a great business. Then I spent all that day and the next in going to the people of my own trade, who worked as hard every day for their bread as I had done. Giving them money beforehand, I engaged them to work for me in different sorts of ropemaking according to their skill and ability, with a promise not to make them wait for their money, but to pay them as soon as their work was done.

By this means I obtained a monopoly of the rope trade of Bagdad and was soon obliged to hire large warehouses. Later, wishing to have more spacious accommodation, I built that house you saw yesterday, which, though it makes so great an appearance, consists, for the most part, of warehouses for my business with apartments absolutely necessary for myself and family.

Some time after I had left my old mean habitation and removed to this, Saad and Saadi came to see how I had fared. To their surprise they learned that I had become a great manufacturer and was no longer called plain Hassan, but Cogia Hassan Alhabbal, and that I had built, in a street which was named for them, a house like a palace.

They immediately set out to congratulate me upon my success; and, as I happened to see them coming, I was able to receive them with a becoming display of gratitude. After we were seated, Saadi said, "Cogia Hassan, pray tell us by what skill you have converted the four hundred pieces of gold I gave you into so great a fortune."

Saad here interposed, saying: "Why do you still doubt our friend? Let him tell us himself to which of us he owes his wealth."

After this discourse of the two friends, I told them every circumstance your majesty has heard, without forgetting the least.

My words were powerless to convince Saadi, who persisted in claiming the honor of having made me rich. And as, when the discussion was ended, it was late, they made ready to depart. But I detained them, saying, "Gentlemen, there is one favor I have to ask. I beg of you not to refuse to do me the honor to stay and take a slight supper with me, also a bed tonight, and tomorrow I will carry you by water to a small country house which I bought for the sake of the air. We will return on my horses."

They courteously accepted my invitation, and while supper was being prepared I showed them over my house and garden, which they admired. But their praises were loudest when we reached the supper room, where everything was provided for their entertainment.

The next morning, as we had agreed to set out early to enjoy the fresh air, we repaired to the riverside by sunrise and went on board a pleasure boat, well carpeted, that waited for us. In less than an hour and a half, with six good rowers and the stream, we arrived at my country house.

I conducted my guests over the house, and afterwards into the gardens, where, at the end of the garden, was a wood of handsome trees.

As we stood watching, two of my boys, whom I sent into the country, ran into the wood and, seeing a nest which was built in the branches of a lofty tree, they sent a slave up to fetch it. The slave, when he came to it, was much surprised to find it composed of a turban, and told the boys to bring it to me.

After I had examined it well and turned it about, I said to my guests, "Gentlemen, have you memories good enough to remember the turban I had on the day you did me the honor first to speak to me?"

"I do not think," said Saad, "that either my friend or I gave any attention to it, but if the hundred and ninety pieces of gold are in it, we cannot doubt of it."

"I am convinced that the gold is here," said I, "for it is very heavy. Before I undo it, however, I beg you to notice its weather-stained appearance, showing that it has been in the tree a long time."

I then pulled off the linen cloth which was wrapped about the cap of the turban, and took out the purse, which Saadi knew to be the same he had given me. I emptied it on the carpet before them, and said, "There, gentlemen, there is the money. I will count it, and see if it be right." I found it to be one hundred and ninety pieces of gold.

Then Saadi, who could not deny so manifest a truth, addressing himself to me, said, "I agree, Cogia Hassan, that this money could not serve to enrich you; but the other hundred and ninety pieces, which you would make me believe you hid in a pot of bran, might."

I vowed that it was not so; and after that no more was said about the matter. We entered the house and had dinner and, in the cool of the evening, rode back to Bagdad in the moonlight.

It happened, I know not by what negligence of my servants, that we were then out of grain for the horses, and the storehouses were all shut up; when one of my slaves, seeking about the neighborhood for some, met with a pot of bran in a shop. He bought the bran and brought the pot along with him, promising to carry it back again the next day. The slave emptied the bran, and dividing it with his hands among the horses, felt a linen cloth tied up, and very heavy. He brought the cloth to me in the condition that he found it, and presented it to me.

I immediately recognized it, and, running to my guests, said, "See, here are the other hundred and ninety pieces of gold." As further proof I sent the pot to my wife, who quickly identified it as the one she had exchanged for the earth.

Saadi readily submitted, renounced his incredulity, and said to Saad, "I yield to you, and acknowledge that money is not always the means of becoming rich."

Saadi would not hear of receiving back the money he had given me, therefore we decided to bestow it in charity. And when the two friends, Saadi and Saad, left on the next day, we had sworn eternal friendship, which has endured ever since.

The caliph then expressed his satisfaction with their story and said that the diamond was now in his treasury, and that he valued it above all his jewels. "And," added he, "bring your friends here that they may see it."

After these words the caliph gave Cogia Hashan, Syed Nouman, and Baba Abdalla leave to depart, having expressed his approval of their histories.

The Merchant of Bagdad

IN the reign of the Caliph Haroun al-Raschid, there lived at Bagdad a merchant whose name was Ali Cogia, a man of moderate means. He lived in the house which had been his father's, independent, and content with the profit he made by his trade. It happened that he had a strange dream for three successive nights. In it a venerable old man came to him, and with a severe look, reprimanded him for not having made a pilgrimage to Mecca. This troubled him much, for he knew that his faith demanded that he should pay his respects to the holy city, and after this vision dared not tarry any longer without performing his duty. He therefore sold off his household goods, his shop, and with it the greatest part of his merchandise, reserving only some articles which he thought he might turn to a better account at Mecca.

Having let his house also, he took his small savings, amounting to one thousand pieces of gold, and put them in a jar, which he filled up with olives, and deposited with a friend who promised to take care of the jar, not knowing what lay under the olives, until he returned. He then joined a caravan which was about to set out and started on his pilgrimage.

Ali Cogia reached Mecca in safety and, having paid a visit to the holy mosques, he thought about disposing of the goods he had brought with him. For this reason he exposed them in the bazaar for sale.

Two merchants passing by, and seeing Ali Cogia's goods, thought them so choice that they stopped some time to look at them; and when they had satisfied their curiosity, one of them said to the other, as they were going away, "If this merchant knew how much he could get for these goods at Cairo he would carry them thither, and not sell them here."

Ali Cogia heard these words and, as he had often heard talk of the beauties of Egypt, he was resolved to take the opportunity of seeing them by performing a journey thither. Therefore, after having packed up his goods again, instead of returning to Bagdad, he set out for Egypt, with the caravan of Cairo. There he very quickly sold his goods at a large profit. With the money he bought others, with an intent to go to Damascus. It was some time before a caravan started, and in the interval he visited all the places of interest around Cairo and on the banks of the Nile. When the caravan was ready, Ali Cogia joined it and, having visited Jerusalem on the way, arrived at Damascus after a satisfactory journey.

Ali Cogia found Damascus so attractive a place, being surrounded by verdant meadows, pleasantly watered, and delightful gardens, that it exceeded the descriptions given of it in the journals of travelers. Here he made a long stay. For several years he journeyed from place to place and at last returned to Bagdad.

All this time his friend, with whom he had left his jar of olives, neither thought of him nor them. But at the time when he was on the road with a caravan from Shiraz, one evening as this merchant was supping with his family, the discourse happened to fall upon olives, and his wife was desirous to eat some, saying she had not tasted any for a long while.

"Now you speak of olives," said the merchant, "you put me in mind of a jar which Ali

Cogia left with me seven years ago when he went to Mecca, and put it himself in my warehouse to be kept for him. What has become of him I know not; though when the caravan came back, they told me he had gone to Egypt. Certainly he must be dead, since he has not returned in all this time, and we may eat the olives if they prove good. Give me a plate and a candle. I will go and fetch some of them, and we will taste them."

The wife tried to persuade her husband not to touch the property of another, but he would not heed, and went to get the olives.

When he came into the warehouse, he opened the jar, and found the olives moldy. To make sure he turned some of them upon the plate, and by shaking the jar, some of the gold tumbled out.

At the sight of the gold the merchant, who was naturally covetous, looked into the jar, perceived that he had shaken out almost all the olives, and what remained was gold coin. He immediately put the olives into the jar again, covered it up, and returned to his wife.

"Indeed, wife," said he, "you were in the right to say that the olives were all moldy, for I found them so. I have made up the jar just as Ali Cogia left it, so that he will not perceive that they have been touched if he should return."

"You had better have taken my advice," said the wife, "and not have meddled with them. God grant no mischief happens in consequence!"

The merchant was not more affected with his wife's last words than he had been by her former, but spent almost the whole night in thinking how he might put Ali Cogia's gold to his own use and keep possession of it in case he should return and ask him for the jar. The next morning he went and bought some olives of that year, took out the old with the gold, filled the jar with the new, covered it up, and put it in the place where Ali Cogia had left it.

About a month after, Ali Cogia arrived at Bagdad. As he had let his house, he alighted at a khan, choosing to stay there till he had announced his arrival to his tenant and given him time to provide himself with another residence.

The next morning Ali Cogia went to pay a visit to the merchant, his friend, who received him in the most cordial manner and expressed great joy at his return after so many years' absence, telling him that he had begun to lose all hope of ever seeing him again. After the usual compliments on both sides on such a meeting, Ali Cogia desired the merchant to return him the jar of olives which he had left with him, and to excuse the liberty he had taken in giving him so much trouble.

"My dear friend," replied the merchant, "do not make apologies. Your vessel has been no inconvenience to me. There is the key of my warehouse, go and fetch your jar. You will find it in the place where you left it."

Ali Cogia went into the merchant's warehouse, took his jar, and after having returned him the key with thanks for the favor he had done him, returned with it to the khan where he lodged. On opening the jar and putting his hand down as low as the pieces of gold had lain, he was greatly surprised to find none. His astonishment was so great that he stood some time motionless; then, lifting up his hands and eyes to Heaven, he exclaimed, "Is it possible that a man whom I took for my friend should be guilty of such baseness?"

He returned immediately to the merchant. "My good friend," said he, "be not surprised to see me back so soon. I own the jar of olives to be the same I placed in your warehouse; but with the olives I put into it a thousand pieces of gold, which I do not find. Perhaps you might have had occasion for them, and have employed them in trade. If so, they are at your service till it may be convenient for you to return them; only

put me out of my pain, and give me an acknowledgment, after which you may pay me at your
own convenience."

The merchant, who had expected that Ali
Cogia would come with such a complaint, had
meditated an answer.

"Ali Cogia," said he, "you agree that you left
a jar of olives with me. Now you have taken it
away, you come and ask me for a thousand
pieces of gold. Did you ever tell me that such a
sum was in the jar? I did not even know that
they were olives, for you never showed them to
me. I wonder you do not ask me for diamonds
and pearls instead of gold. Be gone about your
business, and do not raise a mob about my warehouse"—for some persons had already collected.

These words were pronounced in such great
heat and passion as not only to make those who
stood about the warehouse already stay longer
and create a greater mob, but the neighboring
merchants to come out of their shops to learn
what the dispute was between Ali Cogia and the
merchant, and endeavor to reconcile them. When
Ali Cogia had informed them of his grievance,
they asked the merchant what he had to say.

The merchant owned that he had kept the
jar for Ali Cogia in his warehouse, but denied
that he ever meddled with it, swore that he knew

it contained olives only because Ali Cogia told him so, and requested them all to bear witness of the insult and affront offered him.

"You bring it upon yourself," said Ali Cogia, taking him by the arm; "but since you use me so basely, I cite you to the law of God: let us see whether you will have the assurance to say the same thing before the magistrate."

"With all my heart," said the merchant; "we shall soon see who is in the wrong."

Ali Cogia carried the merchant before the magistrate, where he accused him of having, by breach of trust, defrauded him of a thousand pieces of gold which he had left with him. The judge demanded if he had any witnesses; to which he replied that he had not taken that precaution because he had believed the person he trusted his money with to be his friend, and always took him for an honest man. The merchant made the same defense he had done before the merchants, his neighbors, offering to make oath that he never had the money he was accused of, and that he not so much as knew there was such a sum; upon which he was dismissed.

Ali Cogia, extremely mortified to find that he must sit down with so considerable a loss, protested against the sentence, declaring that he would appeal to the caliph, who would do him justice.

While the merchant returned home triumphing over Ali Cogia, and overjoyed at his good fortune, the latter went and drew up a petition. The next day, observing the time when the caliph came from noontide prayers, he placed himself in the street he was to pass through, holding out his hand with the petition. An officer appointed for that purpose, who always goes before the caliph, came and took it to present it.

As Ali Cogia knew that it was the caliph's custom to read the petitions on his return to the palace, he went into the court and waited till the officer who had taken the petition came out of the caliph's apartment and told him that the caliph had appointed an hour to hear him next day, and then asking him where the merchant lived, he sent to notify him to attend at the same time.

That same evening the caliph, accompanied by the grand vizier, Giafer, and Mesrour, captain of the guard, went disguised through the town, as he often did. When passing through a street, the caliph heard a noise and, mending his pace, came to a gateway which led into a little court, in which he perceived ten or twelve children playing by moonlight.

The caliph, who was curious to know at what play the children were engaged, sat down on a stone bench just by, and heard one of the liveliest of the children say, "Let us play at the court. I will be the magistrate. Bring Ali Cogia and the merchant who cheated him of the thousand pieces of gold before me."

As the affair of Ali Cogia and the merchant had made a great noise in Bagdad, it had not escaped the children, who all accepted the proposition with joy and agreed on the part each was to act. One of them took his seat, with all the seeming gravity of a judge; another, as an officer of the court, presented two boys before him, one as Ali Cogia, and the other as the merchant against whom he complained.

The pretended judge then directing his discourse to the feigned Ali Cogia, asked him what he had to lay to that merchant's charge. Ali Cogia, after a low obeisance, informed the young magistrate of the act, related every particular, and afterwards begged that he would use his authority that he might not lose so considerable a sum of money. The feigned judge, turning about to the merchant, then asked him why he did not return the money which Ali Cogia demanded of him. The feigned merchant alleged the same reasons as the real merchant had done before the judge himself, and offered to confirm by oath that what he had said was truth.

"Not so fast," replied the pretended judge. "Before you come to your oath, I should be glad to see the jar of olives. Ali Cogia," said he, addressing himself to the boy who acted that part, "have you brought the jar?"

"No," replied he.

"Then go and fetch it immediately."

The pretended Ali Cogia went immediately, and returning, feigned to set a jar before the judge, telling him that it was the same he had left with the accused person and received from him again. But, to omit no part of the formality, the supposed judge asked the merchant if it was the same; and as by his silence he seemed not to deny it, he ordered it to be opened. He that represented Ali Cogia seemed to take off the cover, and the boy-judge made as if he looked into it.

"They are fine olives," said he, "let me taste them." Then pretending to eat some, added, "They are excellent: but," continued he, "I cannot think that olives will keep seven years and be so good; therefore send for some olive merchants, and let me hear what is their opinion."

Two boys, as olive merchants, then presented themselves. "Are you olive merchants?" said the sham judge. "Tell me how long olives will keep fit to eat?"

"Sir," replied the two merchants, "let us take what care we can, they will hardly be worth anything the third year; for then they have neither taste nor color."

"If it be so," answered the judge, "look into that jar, and tell me how long it is since those olives were put into it?"

The two merchants pretended to examine and to taste the olives, and declared they were new and good. "You are mistaken," said the young judge; "Ali Cogia says he put them into the jar seven years ago."

"Sir," replied the merchants, "we can assure you they are of this year's growth and we will maintain there is not a merchant in Bagdad but will say the same."

The feigned merchant who was accused would have objected against the evidence of the olive merchants; but the pretended judge would not suffer him. "Hold your tongue," said he, "you are a rogue; let him be impaled."

The children then concluded their play, clapping their hands with great joy, and seizing the feigned criminal to carry him to execution.

Words cannot express how much the caliph Haroun al-Raschid admired the sagacity and sense of the boy who had passed so just a sentence in an affair which was to be pleaded before himself the next day. He withdrew and, rising off the bench, asked the grand vizier, who heard all that had passed, what he thought of it.

"Indeed, Commander of the True Believers," answered the grand vizier, "I am surprised to find so much sagacity in one so young."

"But," answered the caliph, "do you know one thing? I am to pronounce sentence in this very cause tomorrow. The true Ali Cogia presented his petition to me today; and do you think," continued he, "that I can give a better sentence?"

"I think not," answered the vizier, "if the case is as the children represented it."

"Take notice then of this house," said the caliph, "and bring the boy to me tomorrow that he may try this cause in my presence. Also order the magistrate who acquitted the merchant to attend to learn his duty from a child. Take care likewise to bid Ali Cogia bring his jar of olives with him, and let two olive merchants attend."

The next day the vizier went to the house where the caliph had been a witness of the children's play and asked for the master; but he being abroad, his wife appeared thickly veiled.

He asked her if she had any children. To which she answered she had three; and called them.

"My brave boys," said the vizier, "which of you was the judge when you played together last night?"

The eldest made answer it was he; but, not knowing why he asked the question, colored.

"Come along with me, my lad," said the grand vizier, "the Commander of the Faithful wants to see you."

The mother was alarmed when she saw the grand vizier would take her son with him and asked why the caliph wanted him? The grand vizier reassured her and promised that he should return again in less than an hour's time.

"If it be so, sir," said the mother, "give me leave to dress him first, that he may be fit to appear before the Commander of the Faithful."

As soon as the child was dressed, the vizier carried him away and presented him to the caliph.

When they reached the palace the boy was very shy, until the caliph welcomed him. He then ordered the merchants to be brought forward. When they were introduced, they prostrated themselves before the throne, bowing their heads quite down to the carpet that covered it. Afterwards the caliph said to them, "Plead

*"Plead each of you
your causes before this child."*

each of you your causes before this child, who
will hear and do you justice; and if he should be
at a loss, I will assist him."

Ali Cogia and the merchant pleaded one after
the other; but when the merchant proposed his
oath as before, the child said, "It is too soon.   It
is proper that we should see the jar of olives."

At these words Ali Cogia presented the jar,
placed it at the caliph's feet, and opened it.   The
caliph looked at the olives, took one and tasted
it, giving another to the boy.   Afterwards the
merchants were called, who examined the olives,
and reported that they were good, and of that
year.   The boy told them that Ali Cogia affirmed
that it was seven years since he had put them

up, when they returned the same answer as the children who had represented them the night before.

The caliph, fully satisfied of the merchant's villainy, delivered him into the hands of the ministers of justice to be impaled. The sentence was executed upon him, after he had confessed where he had concealed the thousand pieces of gold, which were restored to Ali Cogia. The monarch, most just and equitable, then turning to the magistrate, bade him learn of that child to acquit himself better of his duty; and embracing the boy, sent him home with a purse of a hundred pieces of gold as a token of his liberality and admiration of his acuteness.